The Mindset of Rich and Poor

How poor people think and rich people think

Jo Batiquin

Ukiyoto Publishing

All global publishing rights are held by

Ukiyoto Publishing

Published in 2021

Content Copyright © Jo Batiquin

ISBN 9789364948227

All rights reserved.
No part of this publication may be reproduced,
transmitted, or stored in a retrieval system, in any
form by any means, electronic, mechanical,
photocopying, recording or otherwise, without the
prior permission of the publisher.

The moral rights of the author have been asserted.

This book is sold subject to the condition that it shall
not by way of trade or otherwise, be lent, resold, hired
out or otherwise circulated, without the publisher's
prior consent, in any form of binding or cover other
than that in which it is published.

www.ukiyoto.com

CONTENTS

Introduction	1
You need to be a champion to become rich.	2
If you want to be rich, then work like a rich!	21
The difference between rich and poor	33
You must have an attitude of the rich	46
Live like a rich	63
Investments strategy of the rich	76
You can't be rich by thinking poor	101
Why do poor people have so much debt?	113
How the rich generate their income?	123
Rich people are successful,	129
Poor people are unsuccessful	129
Why poor people are staying poor and broke?	142
Rich people are eco-friendly, poor people are eco-enemies	150
Poor people has scarcity mindset. Rich people have rich mindset	158
Why you must get rich?	164
How poor people struggle with their behaviours?	172
How poor people suffer from hunger?	179
Rich people have a good mentality. Poor people have a bad mentality	187
Poor people are vicious.	196
Rich people have vision	196
Poor people are immature.	201

Rich people are matured 201
Poor people focus on reading social media posts. 208
Rich people focus on reading books. 208

About the Author *217*

Introduction

This book is about poverty and why these two (2) kinds of people are not alike. One of them has more resources, while the other has a limited supply or shortages. I will state why these people most likely have a positive mindset unlike the opposite one; some are struggling financially and others have more freedom. This literature is based on my experiences and observation of their attitude and behavior every time I encounter each one of them.

Some people believe that being rich require fancy cars, mansions, popularity, airplane, and a lot of money. Thus, being rich only demands a good mindset. If your perception is set only for material things, there are times you will lose it. However, when you have a mindset, same as those rich individual; you're not afraid to lose everything. Since, you knew that you can have it back. Being rich is having a heart, mind and soul. It's based on emotion, contribution, and leadership. Even if you have all the money in the world, yet lack proper thinking; you will never call yourself rich. As rich people didn't teach their children the value of money, rather create it with their hands.

You need to be a champion to become rich

Start with what you have

Last night, I was selling '**balut**' (duck egg) door to door to my neighbors. One of them told me that he wanted to sell duck eggs just like what I did. I ask him what's stopping him to sell?

He said, "First, I need to save money to buy a bike, and look for a supplier. I also need to have a big basket, so I can sell more eggs."

"Why don't you start with what you have? I can be your supplier if you want, and some duck egg vendors don't need a bike. They're just walking while selling; communicate with people. Instead of waiting for something that you didn't have, why don't you start with what you have right now? You can walk like what other vendors do. You don't need a bike to start selling as long as you have good communication skills," I stated.

"I need to save more money first to buy a bike. Therefore, I can go to another place whenever I want," he answers.

I just smile at him and leave my last response, "That's a good idea if you had a bike; you can sell anywhere you want."

However, at the back of my mind, I am not agreeing with it. The fact is, poor people are waiting for something before they even start. Same thing as buying a lottery ticket, waiting for news that they're winning. Sometimes people want to do something, but wish for miracles to happen.

Inspiring Story

There's a story about a little girl who runs in an athlete's competition. Everyone's laughing at her shoes, and they call her a beggar. Rhea Bullos is an eleven (11) years old girl who lives in the Philippines. She has done sports since her early childhood. She's from a low-income family who couldn't afford to buy even their basic needs, and sports equipment. Despite of this, she works hard every day; using different kinds of objects to help her. Rhea didn't care when they call her a beggar. All she does is ignore them and continue her goal.

Several years ago, children were recruited from their local school. Rhea expresses her desire to join the competition, yet her parents are stopping her. Considering the thought that her parents can't afford to buy that thing. Thus, she forbids to join.

On December 2019, Rhea took her part in an international school track and field happened in the province of Ilo-Ilo. At the very start of the race, the spectator is already begun to whisper to themselves. They are very suspicious of what they saw. However, the little girl wanted to take part in the competition.

Since she didn't have a single spare of snickers, she found a very unique solution to her problem. She decided to make shoes from medical tape. The young lady tape her entire foot; she even draws a Nike logo on the top. The girl with the medical tape finished 3 races: the 400 hundred meters, 800 hundred meters, and even 15 hundred meters. That's an incredible feat! She took hundreds of competitors on 400 hundred meter race. Then, she passed her opponents on 800 hundred meter race. Later, she conquers the 15km in a 1 half distance. The girl came home with 3 gold medals. The lesson is, ("If there's a wheel, there's a way.")

Listen to no one else voice, but yours.

The universe is surrounded by numerous opportunities (even the pants that you're wearing). But the problem about those poor people, they didn't see it on their minds. They only see them in their eyes and walk away. They're not willing to take the risk, because they're too afraid of rejection, discrimination, and what other people say. They're rational and emotional. They are full of "**what ifs.**" What if it won't work. What if I don't have time for my kids. What if my acquaintance saw me selling on the street; that's awkward and different.

Their mind is preventing them from doing something because they have many "what ifs." The world is filled with people who think they know you. Listen to no one else voice, but yours. If you don't get out of that chain and keep listening to them, you'll be stuck on that chain forever.

"Man is born free and everywhere he is in chains."
—*Jean Jacques Rousseau*

Before you even try something, expect the worst things to happen. Since every decision you made; every action you take; there's something that you cannot control. Just like the poor people around you. They will tell you negative words and pull you down. Some say, "Don't try it. You will fail. " Some will tell, "Play it safe," or "No, you're not good about that!" Others might say, "You're just wasting your time."

The fear and doubts in your mind are the biggest problem. Sometimes we agreed on what they said. You'll respond, "Yeah, they're right," and "I'm not that smart." There's a voice who'll whisper, "I have a horrible memory," and "I'm not that good."

Yeah, you're right. Since what you think is what you become. If you think that you can do it, you're right. But if you think that you can't do it, then you're correct as well. Our thoughts are very powerful. You will turn into what you feed and what you say towards it.

Learn how to feed your mind with positive thoughts, because your mind makes your action; this becomes your results. What you think, is what you do. If you think something negative, then negative starts to happen. If you think you're doing something positive, positive things start to happen. There's a powerful energy that comes from our mind that once you tell the universe what's going to happen, it will give you the energy that comes from your subconscious mind. Those will reflect your action, and it will create the result.

You can be who you are and what you become if you believe in it. There's a lot of choices to pick from, yet you're the only one who could choose the right path that you wish for. You're the only person that can make those things happen.

You live your thoughts, and it will lead you whatever you want in your life. It comes from within, the same as planting trees: first, you need to sow seeds and bear a lot of fruit.

If you want to reap big fruits, what's inside of it will reflect on the outside. How big is your fruit, is the outcome of the seed that you put in.

> Your mind becomes your actions.
> Your action becomes your results.

How sharp is your mind?

The more you sharpen your mind, the more profit it brings such as cutting fruits. The sharper your knife, the more fruits you could sell.

Our mind is the most important thing made by God. Same as Eve when the serpent told her to eat the fruit of knowledge. As soon as she eats it, she realizes that she is undressed. Many people are aware of what they're doing, yet they tend to ignore it. It is due to our educational system right now, and they are not changing.

Education is not the most important thing, since they're focusing on academics. They're not teaching on how making financial literacy. Learning from school is good, but learning from other people's mistakes, and experiences are the best teacher. Poor people in school are more focused on good grades; find a stable job to work, so that you will be secure. Poor people in school after they get their degree, don't want to learn anymore. Somehow for some people, learning from school is just the beginning.

The truth is that God let Eve to eat the fruit of knowledge, so she can learn something new. God wants us to learn, while we're still breathing—still alive. Don't stop learning. If you want to help someone, don't just help financially. Also, teach them mentally. If you only give some money, they can just spend it all. Otherwise, if you give wisdom to someone, it can bring more money.

If you want to help others to succeed, learn to give them the right information. Leaders are not making followers, instead, they make leaders. Rich people have a leadership mentality. Poor people have a follower mentality.

> *"Poverty of goods is easily cured. Poverty of mind is irreparable."*
>
> — *Michel de Montaigne, French philosopher*

Focus on what's important

If you are focusing on your education right now that's good. However, if you only educate yourself to be the best employee, then you're not working on your dreams. You're working for other people's dreams. Even though you're hard working, and a talented employee in the world. If you're just an employed, you're not working on your dreams.

Jack Ma, the richest man in China said that "If you put money, and banana in front of a monkey they will choose banana. Whereas, monkeys don't know that money can buy more bananas. In reality, if you offer jobs and businesses to people, they will choose jobs. Since some individuals don't know that business can bring more money. Salaries can make you a living, but profit can make you a fortune."

If you want to earn more money, then don't just earn— learn. The more you sharpen your mind, the more money you could make. If you want to do what other rich people do, you have to try what you have never done before. Don't just sit on your couch, and wait for a miracle to happen. It's never going to happen. The more you take action, the more your dreams will come true.

The world is filled with smart people, but they're focusing on improving their skills. They're not enhancing their wisdom, and the ability to learn more. This is the reason why more companies are hiring educated people so that they can teach them what to do. Same as educated people who are working with rich people. This kind of person tends to explore and learn the most important things in life. But educated people learn so many things in life.

This morning, I wake up and listened to Bro. Bo Sanchez' power talk. He put 3 ladders on stage, and say, "To become a superstar, you need to choose the ladder where your spirits are."

> *"School days, I believe that this are the unhappiest event in the whole span of human existence. They are full of dull, unintelligible tasks, new, and unpleasant ordinance; the brutal violence of common sense, and common decency."*
>
> —H. L. Mencken

The only key to becoming successful is *"hard work"*

You will get the degree, and find a stable job. If you're not contented with your salary, you'll desire to earn more. Therefore, you'll study again for promotion, and this will take time. The truth is, the key to becoming successful is hard work. You spend a lot of time on your promotion, but you don't spend time educating yourself. Time is the most valuable thing in your life. You lose money, then you can re-earn it. You lose time, you can never redeem it.

That's the reason why I don't spend my lifetime in school. There's a lot of things that I could learn outside of school; the people that I meet on the street every day. In 10 years of studying, school is like talking to an old wise man for 4 hours. The things that I could learn from numerous people and the mistakes that I've made each day are the most important lessons. That's what makes me stronger, and wiser. I can determine who I was. It's better to fail early, so you will know yourself and find the important things in life. When you realize you're doing the wrong thing, that's the best teacher that you could have ever encountered. I've made so many mistakes in the past, yet I don't blame myself. Since, without it, I can never become who I am today. The decision I made in the past is part of my history for tomorrow. I can never bring the past back, yet I can still fulfill my dreams for the future. This will start by making the right decision today.

Some people are just passing by on your life to learn more things, but some poor people are wasting your time by entertaining you. For me, it's better to be with myself, than the other people who don't give value to your life.

"Be ye therefore merciful, as your Father also is merciful."
Luke 6:36(KJV)

Get out of your free lunch

When I was 25 years old, I was addicted to using drugs, alcohol, and cigarettes. I spend my life enjoying it since I have my Mom who supports me. That's the reason why I abuse her money to buy bad habits. I use it in partying, going to the clubs, and hanging out with the people that I hate. Not realizing that my actions never make me grow. I was stuck on the free lunch that can push me by doing bad things every day. There are times that I wanted to get out of my comfort zone; find ways to support myself. Thus, the problem is that I have a Mom who loves me so much that she doesn't even care about the mistakes that I made. As a result, I didn't get the degree in college, due to my free lunch. I didn't grow that way. I study for almost 8 years in college. Only got 2 years graduate of an associate. I waste all the money on my mother.

Powerful Advice

Friends, get out of your free lunch, because you will never grow in the capacity to earn. Learn how to be financially independent, and try to make it on your own. Find ways to survive without the others. Once you didn't change your lifestyle, it will be so easy. As Densel Washington state that, if it's easy, it will become so hard. If it is so hard, then it will become so easy. Living with your parents is good, yet living with your privacy is the best way to start your life. You can create a better version of yourself. Being safe, and secure is not good, especially when you're in reality. Staying in your comfort zone will kill you. Did you know that usually, civilians are the first to get died in the war because they don't know how to fight? All they do is hide, kneel, and beg not to die. It's either, you fight or defend, but if you're always defending you won't conquer the kingdom. Learn how to fight, and conquer the world.

If you want to receive more blessings, then try to make a new living. The more independent we are, the more we believe in blessings. I believe that the best blessing that we receive in our lives is to be financially free. If you're struggling to find jobs, try different things; use social media platforms. You can be a YouTube vlogger, or you can be an online seller. Use your skill if you're good at communication. You can also be a virtual assistant.

There are so many ways to find work. Stop saying that you can't find any. Remember, you're the only person who's responsible for your progress. If you don't change, then who else?

"Delight yourself to the Lord,

and he shall give you the desire of your heart."

—*Sums 37:9*

Choose your friends wisely

"Who you spend time with, is who you become. Change your life by consciously choosing to surround yourself with people with high standards"

—*Tony Robbins*

When I was young, I spend time with these poor friends of mine. I don't care about the important things in life. I enjoy wasting moments with them, because I thought that life is too short. We're just going to die when we get older. I want to cherish every hour, and minute in my life. However, my friends never grow, they're just immature like me. I waste a lot of money by enrolling in universities. Somehow, I only care about the temptation of my poor friends. I don't mind my studies. I thought that I can go back to school whenever I want.

My poor friends told me that it's okay if I fail every semester. There's a lot of changes coming. The school is not running. It was still there whenever you want to go back. At least, you enjoy your life, unlike your classmate. Their life is boring. They didn't enjoy their lives. I hear that advice when I was high on dope.

I believe that I can enjoy my life together with them. Using drugs makes me agree with what they say. At that time, I didn't care about money. I just want to spend it whenever I want to buy dope. As cited by Bob Marley, "Money can't buy happiness." I don't care about savings. I don't know what investing is. Not realizing that I was surrounded by poor people. Even the celebrities that I admire keep saying, "You only live once." Bruno Mars told us, "I wanna be a billionaire, so freaking bad." At first, I thought that money is not important. Money is evil. Money can't buy life.

Until I realize that I'm still stuck in my position. I'm not growing. I failed every semester. I'm still immature. I am the same person as I was yesterday. I'm not changing. My perspective in life depends on the people I follow. I was cursed. I can't get out of my poor mindset. I try to look for a job, but no one wants to hire me. In every interview I was high. The interviewer notices the way I talk and I smell like a weed. I realized that I'm useless. I want to change, but I just can't. Every time I wanted to change, my poor friends out there drag me by doing bad things. I noticed that I only want is to get high. Therefore, I realize that I was stuck on what I've been using every day. So, when I quit drugs, that's the time I change.

Powerful Advice

Friends, get out of that zone as soon as possible. If you are still in that room with lots of distractions. You will be destructed for the rest of your life. The world is full of devastation, and if you belong to them, you will never grow. Unless you we're apart from them. Learn to find yourself. Don't allow yourself to be surrounded by people who don't have dreams. Don't let others control you. What you believe, is what you become. Be careful about what you feed into your mind. You will become what you follow. You will turn on what you eat. You will get what you study.

Make the right decision. It's never too late to start over. Choose the right friends. Don't ruin your life. Surround yourself with positive minded, nourishing, good, and rich people. Be coachable. Find mentors who can teach you whatever you want in life. I know you have big dreams; follow them. Listen to the good people. Be a great person. If you follow those people, you will become one of them.

"Finally, brethren, whatsoever things are true. Whatsoever things are honest. Whatsoever things are just. Whatsoever things are pure. Whatsoever things are lovely. Whatsoever, things are good report; if there'll be any virtue, and if there'll be any praise. Think about these things."

Philippians 4:8 (KJV)

"It doesn't matter where you came from, the matter is who you become.'

Inspiring Story

The story of Kentucky Fried Chicken.

At five, his father died. At fourteen, he dropped out of Greenwood's school. He tried odd jobs working on farmland. Later, as a streetcar conductor. At 16 years of age, he joined the army. Subsequently, he became a railroad locomotive; he quit anyway. At eighteen, he got married. Within the few months of the same day, he was fired from his job. His wife said that she's pregnant; she eventually left him.

Then, he experiences depression. He tries to do work selling insurance, and tires. He also runs a gas station, and drive a ferry boat. Amidst his misery, he remained honest. Try to kidnap his daughter from his former wife, but he failed.

At the age of 65, Harland felt even worthless when he received his first social security check: only 105 dollars. He attempts to commit suicide, because he felt like a loser. However, the table began to turn, when he decided to run a new business. He sat in the park writing in his journal. He has written the old family recipe he had remembered and searched for a restaurant owner who is willing to take his old recipe. He failed 1,007 times. Finally, the 1,008 restaurant owners agree to his proposal. Later on, Harland purchases the restaurant.

The man who had become a kidnapper and a former loser with his entire life was Colonel Harland Sanders.

At the age of five, my father died in kidney failure. We don't have money to bring him to the hospital, so we don't have any choice to stay at home. My mother was so depressed. She went into prostitution for us to survive. When I was in college, my dream is to become a famous musician and songwriter. I've tried to sing in the local bar in Cebu, but I failed. I went to the recording studio to record my songs, but they rejected me.

However, I continue. I spend all of my time writing songs; singing at the local club without any pay. I let go to my school even though I enrolled in the university. I don't care about what others say even they are laughing at me every time I sing on the stage. I failed anyway. I didn't become famous. I did all I can, but I never become a popular songwriter. Maybe, that's God protection. Whenever I play music, I'm near to drugs.

Eventually, when I was scrolling on my Facebook page I saw my batchmate wearing black togas. While looking at their images, there are so many doubts and regrets. I realize that I waste all my energy and effort by doing something impossible. I exchange my education for worthless things. So after 8 years of studying with 2 years graduate in associate vocational, I go back to the province where I grow up. I turn depressed.

At home when I'm alone, I get my blanket and tie it to my neck. I go up in the stairs and ready to jump; to commit suicide. Until, I saw the image of Jesus Christ on the poster in front of me (my mother loves to collect posters of God, and post them on our wall). It is something that I couldn't forget for the rest of my life, even when I get into my deathbed. I was looking for him, while I was rapping myself on the stairs. He whispered something in my ears and said, "Son, you're not done yet."

The tears in my eyes start to drop. As I look at him, I realize how important I am to God. Maybe, I have an important mission that he wants me to accomplish. Those words awaken me. I was reborn. He gives me a second chance to live—to start again. There was something that flash in me. I untied myself and thought that it is not over. I failed so many times, but this is not the end. This is just the beginning.

Eventually, I found a girl with whom I fell in love. She helps me to get rid of drugs, and start finding jobs. I failed 15 times in searching for jobs in Cebu. So my girlfriend brought me to Manila to find possible jobs there. By the grace of the Lord, I was hired in the fast-food chain. I work as a service crew for almost 1 year. Somehow, when the pandemic comes in, I'm one of those who get terminated. After the lockdown, I look for ways to survive, since I don't want to be a sinker to my girlfriend. I sell different kinds of items to survive like: face shield, facemask, bottled water, and many more on the street. After that, she left me. She doesn't want me to be with her anymore since I am poor. I was so depressed at that time, but I let her go. I respect her decision. On that day, I promise myself that I don't want to be poor anymore. I will become rich!

Even though we're apart, I continue my life in Manila. I start investing in the stock market. I buy land property in Bulacan. Build my own small business. I meet many people in my life who help me in my journey.

Don't worry if someone wants to go out in your life. It's a form of blessing. Sometimes, God wants to remove people from your life, so that you can have more time with yourself. Because without pain, there's no gain. Never focus on the pain. Concentrate on the process. Pain is temporary, but hope is forever. You tried different kinds of ways, but failed. However, don't lose hope. The moment you still breathing, there's always something to hold on to.

"I've tried my best and failed. Well, I've tried my best"

—Steve Jobs

Rich Mindset Activity Action Exercise:

1. Get a sheet of paper/journal, and pen. Write down the seven (7) actions in getting out of your free lunch for you to be financially independent. Just like this: I will rent an apartment on my own: I will get out of my parent's house and so on. Take action immediately!

2. List down the five (5) or more ways to support yourself, and earn more money.

3. Write down the names of five (5) or more poor people who only gave a negative influence on your life. Those whom you want to remove, for you to change your life. And start surrounding yourself with rich people.

4. Write down the name of five (5) or more rich people that you want to surround yourself with. And guide you on your journey to fulfill your dreams. Start following them.

5. Join the club to surround yourself with positive and rich people like Go Negosyo, Truly Rich Club, and Kasosyo Malupit Group.

6. Find a personal wealth coach that can teach you every day to achieve your goals.

7. Bend your right arm in front of you, and make a fist with your hand and say this:

I will become rich

One more time.

I will become rich!

One more time.

I will become rich!

say it again and again.

If you want to be rich, then work like a rich!

The Ten Mindset of Rich and Poor

In this section, I'm going to talk about the work ethics of poor and rich people: how they work every day?

1. Rules

❖ Poor people follow the rules, while rich people make rules.

2. Security

❖ Poor people seek job security, while rich people seek better opportunities.

3. Risk

❖ Poor people avoid taking risks, while rich people calculated it.

4. Works

❖ Poor people work for someone else, while rich people work for themselves.

5. Get paid

❖ Poor people get paid for being present, while rich people get paid based on the results.

6. Work Ethic

❖ Poor people work hard, while rich people work

smarter.

7. Earning Money

❖ Poor people exchange their time for money, while rich people focus on money making machines.

8. Taking a vacation

❖ Poor people are looking forward to holidays and vacations, while rich people looking after their daily works with no interruption.

9. Failure

❖ Poor people disliked failures, while rich people overcome failures.

10. Change

❖ Poor people avoid changes, while rich people adopt new challenges.

If you want to become rich, change your mind set by changing your work ethics. Step out of the comfort zone and work like a rich person. Remember, you will never get rich by just getting paid. Rich people are more optimistic, positive, and determinate. They didn't just work hard, instead smart. Therefore they have not filled themselves with negative thoughts. However, the poor continue to think negatively. They often stay in their comfort zone. Rich people are playful; they always move contradicts. They do not stick in one place. They always find ways to achieve something. They're productive, and goal oriented. They don't like to be tied up, but to achieve something every day. Even if you're the busiest person in the world, if you don't earn it, it's worth nothing. Poor people are very busy; they have multiple jobs. Rich people only work in their office.

Poor people die early due to lack of rest. Our body is the most important assets. If you lose it, you can never earn again. Learn how to multiply your resources—not your body. When you become older, you will become weak. Once you turn weak, you will become nothing. If you have not found ways to switch to the rich mindset, therefore, you will be badly dead and broke. If you aren't born rich, that's not your fault. If you die poor, it's your mistake

"If you will not earn while you're asleep, you will work until you die."

—*Warren Buffett*

Don't be a Rat. Be a Superhero.

Poor people prefer jobs security. Their wealthy day is the 30th day of the month: the Christmas is 13th day. Their rest day is Independence Day. Their lives are just like a hamster running in the metal wheel. When you wake up tomorrow, he's still in the cage. As people do every day: wake up in the morning, go to work, get a pay check, go home, sleep and repeat until die.

When you're a kid, you want to be a superhero. You want to have a superpower like Superman. But when we get older, our dream is waiting for the pay check to come at the end of the month. And sometimes we have complaints about this government. (Why did the government deduct such a large amount from my salary?) You know what, before you get your pay check, 30% of your salaries goes to the government.

In the Philippines, if you have worked for minimum wage of 537 pesos for 8 hours, your monthly salary is 16,110 pesos. If you do a calculation multiply the monthly deduction of 30%. Therefore, 4,833 pesos comes from the government per month; less the salary you have. You only get 11,277 pesos per month. Quite good, if you live with your parents. Yet if you have a family to support, I don't think that's enough for you. Imagine, you work 8 hours per day, 48 hours per week, and 192 hours per month for only 11,277 pesos. Where's that dream of yours? You know what, work is a stepping stone to the enterprise of your dreams. So if you want to stick with that and be happy with that salary, you curse yourself. You must increase your financial IQ.

As Allan Greenspan says that the number one problem of today's generation and economy is the lack of financial literacy. If you want to be a superhero, you'd better think like one. Superheroes don't just like to have superpower, but they also have a powerful mind to change the world. Poor people said, "Money is the root of all evil." Still, they work for money every day. How is it that money is bad if you use it for good, if you use it to help others. Do you think you might be able to help if you have a financial problem as well? Instead, you have to say this, "A lack of money is the root of all evil." If you want to become a superhero, use your mind to earn more money. If you want to help others, you must help yourself first.

"In order to know more, do more, and be more. We must have more.

We must have things to use, for we learn and do, and become; only by using things. We must get rich, so we can live more."

—*Wallace D. Wattles*

If there are many doubts about your job, do not complain to the government because you choose to work with them. If you're not satisfied with your income, then you have to be a superhero. Superheroes are forms that think about other people, and you also have the mind to create something better. If you're trapped in the rat race, figure out ways to get out of there. Learn to step out of your comfort zone, for you will never grow up unless you make something from nothing. You know what, 70% of self-made millionaire Americans are starting with low capital. Some start at zero capital. They just sell a product with their friends, and they let them pay for it before they get the product.

How do you define entrepreneur?

Entrepreneurship is a decision making. If you're an OFW (Overseas Filipino Worker) and you want to go back to your home town in the Philippines (you also want to build a business there). But the problem is that you have a current job overseas, so what should you do? The answer is, you must decide. Whether you would like to start a business and go home, or stay in your comfort zone. You could not choose both, because if you want to run a business, you will be the first to manage it. I advise you to never run your business in an automated way. Meaning, don't let other people handle it. You must be on the ground because if you do that, after one year, you are no longer the owner; you are just a financier. Do you think that Tony Tan Caktiong (when he built Jollibee) might let others run his store? No, because he knows how to handle it. Do you believe that for almost 40 years, Jollibee did not go bankrupt once? I guess his first year in Jollibee; he's the cashier; he's the waiter; the cook. He's very hands on. Have you still seen Tony Tan Caktiong around Jollibee right now?

If you're deciding to run a business, go back home (even when you have a capital or not). That's not what you could do to start, but determination and willingness to begin. When I was making money during pandemic, I sell different kinds of items to survive like: face shield, face mask, duck egg and many more. I force myself to sell anything, because I do not have the choice. I want to survive. I am determined and willing to learn. I don't mind about the risk. I just want to survive, because God put me in there. If God put you into a difficult situation, don't say, "Why me?" said, "Try me!" Finding ways of survival and being decisive. There is a time in our lives when the unexpected situation will come. When God put you in there, that's was your calling.

Becoming a superhero is not just starting by gaining strength, it begins with the mindset. The decision you make by gaining power. If you want to go to the gym, the first thing that comes from your mind is, how do you get there. So you need action to do it. (What if your mind is stopping you from going there?) It's impossible to gain the strength that you wish if you ain't moving.

If you want to get out of the cage, first you need to get out of the wheel. It's not hard to start over, but it's so hard to stuck on the cage forever.

I remember the rabbit and turtle running in the marathon. The rabbit runs in line on the road as no one can stop his frenzied. However, when he saw that the turtle was far away—running slowly. He just slept for a moment and took a break. As soon as he wakes up, the race is over.

Poor people are stopping to learn new things because they think they know everything. But some people are willing to learn and take risks, even with slow progress. It's not how hard to finish the race, but how strong we are to finish it.

Inspiring Story

I remember Angelica Bengtsson when she jumped into the pole vault Olympic competition. She broke her pole. Instead of crying like a little girl, she gets up and face the audience with a smile. Eventually, she finds another pole and jump again. She earns the World Youth Championship, and Junior Championship Athletes. Angelica won gold medals.

Champions never stop even if they fall down, they get up and fight back. When there's an obstacle come, they've found their ways to move forward. Much like becoming a superhero, you will first be defeated. But if you're brave enough to survive, you find ways to defeat your enemies. The truth is, you must die first before you actually live.

> *"A champion is someone who gets up when he can't."*
> —Jack Dempsey

Working hard is good, but working smart is better.

I've met a lot of people in my life who don't like their jobs. Once, you ask them about the reason why they don't quit their job, they reply, "I don't have a choice." At times, they pretend to be happy, so their boss didn't fire them. When you apply for jobs do not stick with one company; make more resources; make more resume. When your boss feels like you're loyal to your job, he will take you for granted (because you don't have a choice). Don't try to please anyone. If the person wants to fire you or mock you, let them go. The moment you beg for other people, your value goes down. Stay on high value. Stay on high standards. Treat yourself like a boss. Don't show them that you're afraid of losing a job. Just enjoy what you're doing. If you want to get a promotion, let them know that you are willing to work for it.

Some people are afraid of exploring new things, since they feel comfortable in what they're doing. If the nurse has seen blood, she immediately runs for it; prepares medication. But if you ask the nurse an opportunity, she runs away. She's afraid of you. Somehow, when I see blood, I don't run. I ignore it and move on, because I have a lot of work to do.

Doctors know how to do fix brain problem; do you know how to do brain surgery? It's so hard, if you can imagine. But, there are doctors who do not know how to deal with money problems.

Seventy percent (70%) of employees are not satisfied with their jobs due to low salaries. However, they don't even realize that the opportunities that come their way lead to higher salaries. An employee work hard to get a pay check, but entrepreneurs working hard to get a profit. But how is it that the entrepreneur works in the office with air conditioning, while employees work so hard with their sweat, blood and tears with low salaries?

The Secret of an Entrepreneur

Entrepreneurs know that salaries cannot make them rich, so they must work smarter. They're not afraid of opportunities. Since, if you're afraid of opportunities, then you're scared of becoming rich. Becoming rich comes from opportunities. You cannot imagine any idea if it is not an opportunity. If you avoid the good chances, you avoid the money that comes from you. Learn how to take calculated risk. You must be open to new things. If a glass is filled with water, you can't fill it unless you empty it. Friends, empty your glasses. How can I show you wisdom, if you don't empty your glass?

Entrepreneurs are focusing on making more money using other people's time. In other words, they make money making machines using their businesses, their paper assets, and their real estate. They hate it when they say, "save for a rainy day." They used to tell this, "save for sunny days." Emergency funds are important. However, if you save all your money in the bank for an emergency (with a low interest rate), you'll be broke by the time you get old. Instead, put your 30% or 50% on your investment with high interest rate. Once you put your entire savings in the bank, you seem to be putting yourself in your graveyard.

Working on the Street

Working on the street is very difficult and the most unsafe workplace; bad guys are out there. To me, that's one of the most dangerous jobs in the world. Especially in the poverty zone where plenty of drugs, fraternities, gangs, rapes and wars. Many times, I encounter trouble on the street while selling balut (duck egg). Even so, I prefer to understand these poor people for the sake of my dreams. Most of my customers are under the influence of alcohol, drugs and other things; it absorbs their mind. It's hard to handle sober people, because you can't understand them.

I experience a lot of trouble with drunken people. Especially poor people, you can't control what they'll do to you. Besides, they carry an illegal weapon. Sometimes they're out of their mind and you can't control it. When that incident happened, I walked away for the sake of my life; I don't want trouble.

Whenever I meet poor people in the street, I want to help them. Either way, it's so hard to deal with them if they're under the influence of something. All you need to do is go away and see another customer. At times, I encounter gangs and fraternities; they're killin' each other. That was very threatening because many of them were carrying dangerous weapons. It's risky to sell on the street, your life is God's most precious gift. And if you die with no purpose, I guess that was my time.

I can't forget this incident while I was walking on the street carrying my basket. I was hit by the other guy with a hardwood in my back, and it was so painful I get into the hospital because of that.

Eventually, I never go back to that place anymore. So many poor people you encounter every day of your life. But be grateful of what God gives you, because some of them, they're not happy with their lives. Their minds are very difficult to handle, all you need to do is to understand those poor people for the sake of your life. You can never help them; all you need is to walk away with them.

Rich Mindset Activity Action Exercise:

1. Write down five (5) ways to get out of the rat race or your current job. Start changing your own journey and get out of your comfort zone for you to become rich.

2. List down your fashion or talent that you're good at. Focus on it and start making money out of it.

3. Make a list of the ten (10) things you could do to start making more money, even if it's small. Just like: I want to sell gadgets online: I want to sell vegetables at a market and so on.

4. Choose one of the best on the list that you want to start right now, and execute it immediately. Write down ten (10) opportunities or ideas that may solve

problems for a lot of people. Find ways on how you can execute it.

5. Bend your right arm in front of you and make a fist in your hand and say this:

I will become rich!

One more time.

I will become rich!

One more time.

I will become rich!

say it again and again.

The difference between rich and poor

Some people are not getting rich, because they think that rich people are greedy and selfish. Which is why they hate to make money, since they always assumed that rich people are bad and evil. They believe that the reason they become rich is by doing bad things such as crime, killing others for money, and stealing from someone. They do not realize that most crimes happen in their area, including drugs, sexual violence and poverty.

They still believe that they know everything. Somehow, rich individuals are always listening; ready to learn something new. Poor people often think that all the money in the world belongs to rich people. That is why these people are poor and have no money. The poor wants to give when they have extra money, but they have never had an extra money. However, the rich give in spite of their lack of money. Considering that rich people believe that in order to multiply your blessing, you must give first. They assume that it will bring them 10 times as much as they give. In other words, they give if they have need.

The poor have a victim mentality. They believe that life is unfavorable to them, and they complain so much about it. Whereas rich people are always taking action. They know that every success starts with doing something. They are grateful for what they have received. Poor people are so hard to deal with in terms of selling. If you sell something to them, they immediately say it's too expensive. They can't afford that. While the rich enjoy negotiating and talking to others. They're friendly and ready to help. If you ask them to purchase a product, they answer: How can I afford it? They find ways to buy the items.

Poor people love talking about themselves—their achievements. It's how great they are. They are self-centered, and always hungry for attention. While rich people are grateful and don't talk about their accomplishments. To them, their achievements are the fruit of their sacrifices, and the action of the past. They are blessed and want to bless others.

Poor people have crab mentality. They love to talk about other people. They don't want others to succeed. If they see successful people, they bring them down. They're insecure and jealous. However, rich people talk about ideas. They have a positive mind that can deal with problems. They don't have time to talk about other people. When they see unsuccessful people, they are ready to help them to be as successful as they are.

Poor people often watch entertainments like TV shows. They always spend their time entertaining themselves. Otherwise, rich people always read books. They love educating themselves.

They adore watching educational and motivational programs.

The poor always blame everyone else for their misfortune. They always blame the government, their parents, their boss, the city, the country, friends and pets; it's always somebody else; that's not always their fault. Remember, persons who blame are lame people. Unlike rich people who take responsibility for their failure. For them, failure is part of the process. In order to be successful, they must be willing to fail.

Poor people's priority is saving, while rich people's priority is investing. Why saving for your older self if a penny you earn remains a penny? You don't have to save it forever, because each year our money changes; our economy still prints new money. The inflation rate is changing every year. Your money will not increase its value; it will decrease. Saving is priceless, yet investing is greatness.

"I call heaven and earth to witness against you today; that I have set before your life and death; the blessing and the curse. So, choose life, so that you may live: you and your descendants."

—*Deuteronomy 30:19 (NASB)*

Poor people have lottery mentality

Poor people think that in order to get rich, one must buy a lottery ticket. They rely upon their lives to win the lottery. They have 'get rich-quick mentality'. But did you know that 60% of lottery winners, they are broke after 1 year or 3 years and had debts. Before, when they didn't play the lottery, they didn't have any debts; when they won, they went into debt. Due to the reason that their 'psychological wallet' is very low. If they increase their income, they are not comfortable with it. Their mind is not used to handle big amounts of money. When they increase their income, they just know how to spend it.

For example, you used to have a salary of 10,000 pesos a month, and then you get promoted. Let's say, you will become a manager, your salary increases to 20,000 pesos. Somehow, your 'psychological wallet' is not increasing since you used to have a 10,000 pesos per month. All you do is spend it till it goes back to 10,000 pesos, and again, you spend the rest of it. Before, you drink a 3n1 coffee every day, but you are not a crew anymore (you are promoted to manager) so you increase your lifestyle. You used to simply drink 3n1 coffee, but now you drink at Starbucks. Previously, you settle for an ordinary shirt, but you're a manager right now, so you buy branded clothes. You used to sit in a jeepney, but now you have your own car.

So, after 1 year, you go bankrupt and go into debt. Since your lifestyle is increasing, yet your psychological wallet is not. Your mind isn't trained to handle the big amounts. As with the lottery winners, after winning, they got into debts and turn poor again. Because they're not practicing how to increase their psychological wallet.

Why learning from school is not so important?

"Founding fathers, in their wisdom, decided that unnatural strain on their parents. So, they provided jails called school, equip with tortures called education."

—John Updike

Our school system teaches us little about money. They're just focusing on calculus and how to make a business plan. They are not teaching us how to manage our own money. Business plan is important for a business, but I'd rather had to take more executions. Some companies hired people to make their business plan, saying that education is the key to become successful; so, they can hire many people. But for me, the business model is much more important than the business plan. The business model is the mechanism through which the company generates its profit, while the business plan is a document presenting the company's strategy and expected financial performance for the years to come.

If schools teach us how to make money, and the system that can generates more money to build our own business, some people will focus on how to grow their business. Do you think you stay in a company when your profit is high as your company you use to work? Of course, you will resign and focus on your own company. However, the problem is that some people do not know how to manage the business; we only know how to handle salary. If the school teaches us how to run our own business and how to make investments, our economy is growing faster. More and more investors can invest in our market, because our market is growing; it's getting larger and better. The stronger our economy, the more it becomes healthier. As the world concentrates on local and foreign investments of the

Philippines, foreign investors want to have a piece in our market. Unfortunately, some Filipinos don't get a share of our market, because the school doesn't teach us how to grow and protect our money.

The Edgewater Beach Hotel

I've heard the story of a lot of people who once were successful, but failed in life.

In 1923, at the Edgewater Beach Hotel in Chicago, which is where the eight (8) world's wealthiest financiers met. Those eight men were in control of more money than the U.S. government at the time. These are:

1. Jesse Livermore

❖ He was the greatest "bear" in the wall street; he committed suicide

2. Leon Fraser

❖ He was the president of the bank of International Settlement; commented suicide.

3. Ivan Kreuger

❖ He was the head of the greatest monopoly. He committed suicide

4. Charles Schwab

❖ He was the president of the largest independent steel company. He has lived on loans for five years of his life, and was died penniless.

5. Arthur Cutten

❖ He was known as the greatest wheat speculator in the past. He died insolvent.

6. Richard Whitney

❖ He was the president of the New York stock exchange. He sent to Sing Sing prison.

7. Albert Fall

❖ He was the member of the president Warren G. Harding's cabinet. He was pardoned for his death at home.

8. Howard Hopson

❖ The president of the biggest North American gas company. He went insane.

Some people, when they get rich, they are afraid to lose their money. They avoid what other people say. This is why they pay so much attention to their money. But you know what, if you're really careful handling with your money and when you lose it, you're going to be frustrated.

Inspiring Story

I remember the story of Mr. Chapman. He worked as a junk dealer. He earned his living by collecting what others had thrown away. As the years went by, Mr. Chapman grew old and stopped working. One day, soon after the World War II, he passed away. Since he lived alone and had no closed relatives, the police entered his house to take stock of his possession. They found the house with old furnishings and assorted memorable from Mr. Chapman's history. However, most of their amazement, the police also discovered more than a hundred thousand dollars ($100,000) in an old bill wrapped in boxes all over the house.

The following day, the Toronto Daily Star published a front-page article about Mr. Chapman, in which it asked the obvious question: Why would someone worth more than $100,000 choose to keep their money hidden in old boxes throughout their house?

Why would Mr. Chapman choose to live like a pauper, when he had so much money at his disposal? He would have been able to use his money for his own pleasure. He could have invested it to earn return and help to create jobs for many people. He could have just deposited it into the bank and earned less interest with his money. Instead, he chooses to put it into a "jar on the shelf," and he thereby rendered it absolutely useless.

Whatever you want to do with your money, don't make the same mistakes that poor old Mr. Chapman did.

We use money as a tool to buy things to improve our lives. So, if you keep it forever, and don't circulate it even though how much it is, you'll never get better.

But if you want to have a lot of money to be able to help more people, you won't regret even when you're in your death bed. The reason for which God will bless you, is that you may be blessings for others. When you care about helping and giving, God will provide you more wisdom. If your life runs only for money, they will come at a time when you'll run out of money. Once your money is gone, you are forced to borrow. However, when you are a good person and you come to a point where you will run out of money, people will help you without expecting anything in return. What you give is more than you receive. Some people are more successful, because they use their wealth to prosper others. Just like King Solomon, the wealthiest man who ever lived on the planet earth. He don't prayed money from God, instead "wisdom".

Here's an example, try to remove all the money of Donald Trump. Eventually, you go back to him after 1 year; he's a millionaire again.

If you do not know how to educate yourself by earning money, it is so difficult to overcome when you are in the situation of obtaining money. If you don't know how to handle small amount, it's so hard to manage bigger amount. If you do not appreciate a small quantity, you do not appreciate the greater quantity. Every big start with small, just like numbers. You can't have 10 without 1; there are no 100 without 10; there are not 1000 without 100; there's never a million without one. If you have a patience to succeed you have to start with 1. The reason some rich people do not overcome their failures, because they jump in a huge amount. Do not complain if you start with a small amount as a gigantic company starts on what it has. The lessons and experiences you had by holding a small amount, is better than a big amount.

"The goal isn't more money; the goal is living life on your terms."

—*Chris Brogan*

Poor people play gambling, while rich people play investing.

Last night, when I was hanging out with my neighbors, I open the topic about my real estate investment: my land property in Bulacan. I purchased it nine months ago. I tell them, "You know what, the best investment is property, and land. Considering that it doesn't depreciate its value. It's always increasing. The higher the demand, the higher the value. As the population increases, the value of the land increases as well. Unlike in the house and lot, if they had an unexpected tragedy, it will destroy the house. In land, even if there's an earthquake, tsunami, or tornado it will not crash since its land. More and more humans live in the world, but the land never increases their quantity. Have you ever seen the land getting pregnant? No, right? It's always increasing the value. Unlike in the stock market, once its paper and system crashed, your investment will crash too.

Moreover, I also tell them about Crypto Currency. I have heard that there is a new game in crypto like Axie Infinity. Then I ask them to try to play the game, because it's amazing; you can win crypto while you're playing. Thus, I noticed that I'm the only one who understands what I'm talking about. Seems like, they have no idea what is going on in the world. The other guy encourages me to play online sabong (online cock fighting) since he earns some money. I asked him if he have already lost in this game. He says, "Yes, many times."

Therefore, you're not earning money. You're losing it. The moment you win, your dopamine will be released; this will increase your emotion. You will become greedy. Even if you already win, you'll play again; the result is that you lose. It was like a drug. Once you take it, you will search for more; it wasn't enough for you.

Inspiring Story

I've heard the story of Jang Sam Hyun or also known as Mr. Chang. He was the owner of Korea's largest construction company and traveled to the Philippines. He lost 300 million pesos, all of his profit, buildings, hotel, and apartment. He sold it as a result of the casino. After he loses, he sells Korean noodles down the street in Las Piñas. Many people helped him to recover, and overcome his failure (even my idol, Hungry Syrian Wanderer). However, he betrayed him. He's asking Mr. Chang for ten percent (10%) of his casino gambling earnings.

Once you're a gambler, you're always a gambler. You need to change your mind set in order for you to change your life. If you play casino, the dealer is always the winner. I've seen a lot of people wasting their money on it, especially poor people. Even in my neighborhood, I saw many of them playing online cock fighting; seems like their daily habits. They come up with ways to play gambling, they sell everything on their home to win the game. As soon as they lose in the last game, they work hard to win the game. But the fact is, people are gambling because they want to get rich quick.

You know what, if you always think to get rich quickly, you will always get scammed. If someone's offer you to invest with them and they promise its guarantee; tomorrow or next week you can get the return of 20%, it's totally a scam. The reason why many Filipinos get scammed, because they have no idea what they are getting into. They don't study first before they even enter. If they heard they can get real quick money, they become greedy and aggressive. It's not bad if you become greedy. For me greed is good, because we need a little greed to achieve something. However, you need to think twice. You need to take calculated risks. Control your emotions, and don't get into something that you don't understand. You need to ask someone first, either your colleagues or someone that could trust. Don't hesitate to ask questions; use the FAQ (Frequently Ask Questions.)

Rich Mindset Activity Action Exercise

1. List the ten (10) poor mindsets you are dealing with and are currently facing. This could pull you back every day of your life. Also, indicate the negative beliefs that you want to remove for you to become rich.

2. Make a list of the ten (10) richest mindset that you want to achieve. Push yourself to become

successful in life. Believe in yourself that you can achieve this, and work on it every day.

3. Write a short paragraph on exactly why becoming rich is important to you. Be specific.

4. Make a list of the five (5) or more ways to go out of the gamblers attitude, and change it to the investor's attitude. Just like this: I'll save my money instead of gambling: I will not go to the casino anymore: I will not search any gambling site anymore.

5. Write down the lottery mentality that you have right now. Promise yourself that you won't buy any lottery ticket anymore. Remember, you cannot save any amount of money if you stay in this attitude. If you don't want to change your mindset, you'll depend your future with that ticket for the rest of your life.

6. Bend your right arm in front of you and make a fist in your hand and say this:

I will become rich!

One more time.

I will become rich!

One more time.

I will become rich!

say it again and again.

You must have an attitude of the rich

The Ten Characteristics and Values of Poor and Rich People

1. Poor people value themselves, while rich people value others.

❖ Poor people are selfish. They always think about themselves. Anything they want is for themselves only, and for their own good. But rich people often think about helping others; how to solve their problems; how they can contribute to someone else. They want to build a community to help more people.

2. Poor people value money more, while rich people value time.

❖ Poor people are desperate. They do whatever they want to get money; even if it is illegal. But rich people find ways to multiply their time, that is why they hired individuals to use their time to multiply their income.

3. Poor people value security, while rich people value freedom.

❖ Poor people work for benefits. They always

depend on the government for their retirement. Somehow, rich people have acquired investments, businesses and assets for their retirement. Therefore, they can relax when they get old.

4. Poor people value active income, while the rich people value passive income.

❖ Poor people often seek job security. They're always expecting government assistance. While rich people acquire assets and investments, so that they have no tax or less.

5. The poor enjoy seeking for help, whereas the rich enjoy how they can help.

❖ The poor people are always waiting for someone to help them, but rich people are taking steps to help them.

6. Poor people value entertainment, while the rich people value excellence.

❖ Poor people are always valued by new trends and television shows, while the rich people enjoy new business and investment.

7. Poor people value attention, while rich people value how to become successful.

❖ Poor people are always out of the street to seek validation and attention, while rich people strive for excellence.

8. The poor value complaints, whereas the rich value action.

❖ Poor people always complain about the

government. They say, "walang ayuda," or having no grocery gift packs. While rich people don't care about ayuda, they'd rather take responsibility for themselves.

9. Poor people loves spending while rich people value investing.

❖ Poor people have YOLO mentality (you only live once). They always spend what they get, while the rich people save their money to invest.

10. Poor people value how to get money while rich people value how to make money.

❖ Poor people work hard to get a salary, while rich people work smart to make a profit.

For whosoever will save his life shall lose it, but whosoever shall lose his life for my sake and the gospels, the same shall save it.

—Mark 8:35 (KJV)

If you want to be rich, be humble, and treat people with respect.

I have met many rich people in the past, some of whom are very humble; many of them are very successful. There was a time I met the owner of our school (the moment when I went to school to college). He is a very humble man and I was shocked that the man who approached me is the owner of 4 universities and hotels. Asking something about an ordinary man like me. It felt like an unforgettable moment in my life, because he wanted me to come into his office for lunch. It was amazing that this rich man invited me out for lunch. So, I went to his office to have dinner with him, and we have an unforgettable conversation that you can't hear with an average man. He asks so much about life, but he told me something I can't forget. He said, "Being successful is not based on status; its base on how you can contribute. Even if you don't have wealth right now, but if you desired to help you can call yourself successful." I saluted the fact that this rich old man has a good personality. And he does not choose a selected person, even if you are poor or rich.

Inspiring Story

The Audrey Mosey's Story

The Mosey family spent most of their lives in Yorkshire. In the '50s, in the last century, a young man named Ken proposed to a beautiful woman named Audrey; she said yes. At first, their family life is most likely the same as the others. But a few years later, the couple knew they'd never had children. For various reasons, Ken and Audrey never had a kid. However, despite of this unfortunate news, the couple didn't despair. They vow to live their lives to each other; that's exactly what they did. Ken had a small business for himself, and Audrey supported her beloved husband.

Overall, it was an ordinary family.

The couple travels together. Took an active part of their lives by traveling as they live simply. Everyone knew that the couple were kind and passionate and that they always helped others. However, no one can imagine what the couple is hiding. Ken and Audrey had been together for 60 years, till one day Ken passed away. Friends and neighbors try to cheer Audrey up, but the old woman is always kind and passionate. A few years later, Audrey also passed away at the age of 91. The whole street grave over them loses, and days later, some very unexpected things started to happen.

The thing is, after Audrey passed away, the school and local charities began to receive large donations. Nobody can understand where the money comes from, and who this rich manufacturer is. And it turns out that this money came from the Audrey Mosey's fund. The locals were quite shocked that the founder of the foundation was her; the same Audrey who spent her whole life with her husband in a small, modest house— driving an old car. They have never shown that they have so much money. As they turn out to be the couple with expensive real estate in Barcelona and England.

Instead of living a rich lifestyle and spending money on expensive things. They choose to live a simple life, and enjoy each other. The only person who knew Audrey's wealth was their executor, Paul Layne. He told the couple's decision. Moreover, he claims that the last will of the couple did not surprise him. After all, they've always been a big heart because even everyone knows it. They secretly help out those in need.

Even throughout their lives, they create charities and help children and the poor. "I will do everything to fulfill her last wish," said the man. Audrey had millions of dollars in savings (on her bank account), and they also had money in their husbands' account. It turns out later that she promised to give all the money to the local charities within their town. The couple had this idea when they knew they weren't going to be able to have a child. So, they decided to help people in extremely difficult life situations.

> *"The highest use of capital is not to make more money, but to make money do more for the betterment of life"*
>
> *— Henry Ford*

Be a good businessman

When you are in sales, our customers/clients are our valuable assets, because without them we cannot make a profit. If you're not respecting your customers and treating them properly, do you think they will buy to you again? For example, you have a friend who always annoys you; always treats you as a loser, and does not support you when you achieve something. He also laughs at you every time you encounter a bad situation. Do you still want to be with him? Same as your customer, if you don't treat your customers the way they are special, they won't be with you anymore.

Learn how to value people even your staffs. If you want to achieve something, give value first. If you want to increase the quality and quantity of your rewards, you should increase the quantity and quality of your contribution. The more you give, the more you receive. The more you achieve something, the more you become a better person.

> *"If you want to change the way people respond to you, change the way you respond to people."*
>
> —*Timothy Leary*

If you can't change your poor mentality, you can't change your poor attitude

Poor people are very arrogant. They always think they're God; as if they know everything. They're close minded. They're not approachable; always hate people. They're often opinionated; want to speak to the world about their opinions; about government; about sports; about society; about everything around them.

But rich people continue to learn, to be coachable, and still ask questions. They're willing to learn—they listen. They read books. But poor people always seek attention, validation and never read books. When was the last time these people read books? 10 years ago, 20 years ago, or never? Poor people always speak bad words like: "puta" (bitch): "gago"(stupid): "bubu"(morons).

On the other hand, rich people are careful with their words. Since every word is very powerful. Once you said something negative, you can never change it. They are the words of wisdom, kindness, humbleness, integrity, and generosity.

Poor people always depend on the government such as 'ayuda' (grocery gift packs). They expect assistance from governments. But the rich people are not dependent on the government; they are independent; they're responsible. They are willing to work whatever it takes. They don't care about the governments' ayuda.

Poor people want early success

Poor people are impatient when it comes to making money. They don't like the idea of working hard. They still think they can get easy money for being lazy, which is why they are always get scammed. They believe that in order to get money, they have to rely on others or on selling illegal things. Poor people are always saying that, "Ang yabang naman nito. Umasenso lang, lumaki na ang ulo." (He gets arrogant, because he's been successful. At the same time, his head grows.)

That's why there's nothing happening with their lives, because they always hate being successful. Unfortunately, some of them are your closest friends, and they know you really well. They only want to bring you down; want you to live up to their level. They always say, "You should be happy with what you got."

Sometimes they tell you, "You have changed" or "I do not know you anymore." They're so envy, when someone gets successful.

You know what, you can't change the butterfly if you always stay a caterpillar. The butterfly changes when they start to spread their wings to use it on how to fly. Either way, the caterpillar never changes if she just knows how to use her legs to crawl.

Relationship doesn't matter

If you start your own business, 70% of your relatives and friends won't support you. Except, if you grow up with a family who have business background. But when you start a new job, 90% of your friends and relatives are going to support you. They will expect that you will be ready to settle down, and later gets married.

Poor people always think that if you get to your certain age, you must get married. The problem of our today's society is that we tend to believe that the only thing to accomplish your life is to get married and have a family. Yet did you know that most successful celebrities, artists, CEOs and professionals are single and never get married.

If you are a teenager at this time and have a plan to become a successful businessman, thus your girlfriend gets pregnant. Can you still fulfill your dreams? Of course the answer is, Yes! But not so much, because your resources were divided. Imagine, if your single and focus on fulfilling your dreams, there's a very big chance that you can fulfill all your dreams. Given that you are the only one who has benefitted from your resources.

I failed so many times in my life, even in my past relationship. Still, I don't prioritize the relationship. Ever since, I know once I'm settling in and getting married, there is little chance that I cannot achieve my dreams, because I have an obligation to support. You know what, being single is a lot happier than being in a toxic relationship. Eighty percent (80%) of the relationships, they're not happy together. Especially when you don't make more money, as most breakups are due to financial issues.

Some say, you can't do this on your own. But you know what, by being alone right now, I had a lot more time to myself. My focus is on me and my dreams without any distractions. Therefore, there's a big chance that I can fulfill all my dreams. You don't need someone in your life, as long as you're happy for what you're doing. Be contented of what you are right now. I'm not saying, "don't get into relationship." All I'm trying to say is, if God allows you time to focus on yourself, focus on it. If anyone wants to get out of your life, then let her go; respect her decision. Remember, you're here to survive, not to be with someone. Be a lone wolf. A wolf can survive in the forest without anyone manipulating him. A wolf can hunt food with his own.

May God decide when to give you the right person. Don't settle down if you don't achieve something. When the right time has come and you are ready for that, God will provide. If that never happens, it's okay. Just live and be happy. Focus on being rich. You don't have to force yourself to be with anyone. If you're still chasing women, your value will be reduced. Stay on the high standard. Stay on high value. Just be with yourself. There's a lot of people in this world today. Our population is growing more and more. Humans exist in this world. So, do not worry if you are feeling alone right now, because the truth is that you are not alone. You're not focusing on fulfilling your dreams.

According to the gender ratio in the world.

In 1957, there were more females than males. Worldwide, the ratio of men to women has increased from 99,692 in 1950 to no more than 101,704 in 2011. It is now expected to decline to 100.296 in 2010.

We humans are created to spread across the Universe. Each day, there are new born women, no need to chase them. Don't be a simp. Stop putting emoji heart to a woman. You're just making the woman's head bigger. You can't possibly not have one of those 101% women. If someone wants to go out with your life, it means she doesn't love you. Be with someone who accepts you. But if you're a woman, I suggest you stick with your husband. Don't listen to those feminists. Because I believe that in every relationship, women are always initiated to break up. We men are so faithful. Women are emotional. They were always in touch with their emotions. Men are logical, we've always followed the right path. If your boyfriend/husband initiated a breakup, or he transfers to another woman, that's not a real man. Real men cannot separate from a woman without any reason. If your premium years will fade, it is so difficult for you to have a man when you are getting much older. Do not destroy your family just because feminism thought that you: Feminism is widespread in the Philippines; that which is said to be wrong.

A penny saved is a penny earned

Sometimes when I walk down the street, I see so many pennies on the ground. They're wasting every single penny. Otherwise, they don't realize that if every penny you keep in the bank, it's a great help with your savings. Imagine if you got a 1,000 penny that's equivalent to 250 pesos. If you put it in the bank, say, 20-25 cents a day in the bank, which equals five pesos. If 20 penny coins per month you get 150 pesos per month. Within one year, you have 1800 pesos a year inside your bank. This is a great help on your savings if you want to save more money. If you want to deposit money to the bank, the bank's interest rate is 0.5% annually.

For example, if you place 25,000 pesos now, after a year you have 150 pesos for 0.5% interest rate. As a result, your total amount on the bank after 1 year is 25,150 pesos. If you have over 20 penny coins deposit at the bank for 0.5% interest rate. This is a large saving on your bank account. If you put these 1,800 pesos every year on the stock exchange with an interest rate of 12%, after 40 years you will become a millionaire. But the issue is, 1,800 pesos penny is enough for you to invest each year in the stock market? You invest more.

I have seen many people waste penny on the streets and many of them are poor. Poor people don't value every single penny. When asked if they have a bank account, they reply, "No. I don't have. My entire money is in my pocket." However, when you ask them if they have an investment, they say, "I don't know what it is."

The reason why poor people are always broke, because they don't value the small amount. To them, it is a small amount and a no value. You know what, if you don't value every single amount, you don't value big amount as well. Once you always put yourself in the big amount, there was a time that the big amount that you're holding on, will go back to the small amount.

I saw many people on the street especially poor people, they habit the throwing of penny. Sometimes it's not just one penny but too many. Imagine, if they throw 250 pennies, that is equivalent to 50 pesos. If you place it into gcash with a 5% interest rate on their ATRAM funds, you get 52.5 pesos after a year. However, the question is, 50 pesos per year is enough for you to invest in gcash? You have to invest more.

Learn to value the small things in your life because all we have in the world starts with small; just like when you're a small child.

Trees don't grow without a seed. Humans don't grow unless we start as a child. Animals don't grow up when they don't start as babies. The money doesn't grow when they don't start with the penny.

"It's not how much money you make, but how much money you keep.

How hard it works for you, and how many generations you keep it for."

—*Robert Kiyosaki*

Why being poor is not really good?

I have known many times when I was selling balut (duck egg) in the street while carrying my basket; people will not treat you well. Ang pangit ng tingin sa atin ng mga tao 'pag mahirap ka lang. (People will look at you in shame when you're poor.) Sometimes when you ask them a question, they ignore you. You are, as it were, invisible, particularly in the area of poverty when you sell goods. When they ask how much is your egg, they will easily get angry if they know the price even if you are not doing anything wrong. It's so hard when you live in the poverty area where people are so disrespectful. They always say bad words like "Putang-ina ka!" (Your son of a bitch!) Even if you don't do something and most of them live in poverty area.

Poor people are so arrogant when you don't dress right; they make you ignorant. They assume they know everything than you. The fact of the matter is they are more ignorant than they think. They seem to know you better than you, and some of them seem to be rich. However, some rich people I meet simply dress up even their home is a mansion and they also treat you well. You feel like a human being to them, but the poor in the area of poverty are so difficult to manage; they are godly. They should be humble, for their situation is very complicated. Still, they are more arrogant than rich people. Since rich people are so humble. It's easy to deal with, sometimes you want to be shy because of their good Samaritan. On the other hand, poor people dress well. They have a lot of jewelry on their bodies, but they put fingers on you. They don't realize that they have nothing to be proud of. They feel like they've got everything, even if they're actually poor. Rich people have everything in life, but they have stayed humble.

Why poor people are always broke?

The poor people I meet all the time will tell me: I have no money, I am poor. I don't have enough money to buy. The reason they remain broke and poor is that they don't believe they can make more money if they act. Some of these do not do well in their lives. They're always on the street every morning until night. That's why they complain over and over again about not having any money. Some of them believe that money can wait without any action. They say that they're getting some money. It's as if they're expecting a miracle. You don't wait for money, you must make money. Money will never run to you, you need to catch them by taking actions.

"The price of success is hard work, dedication to the job at hand."

—Vince Lombardi

Rich Mindset Activity Action Exercise

1. Create a financial freedom jar in your home. Deposit money there each day. Either five (5) pesos, one (1) peso, or a single penny, and all you lose change.

2. Write down the new everyday habit of changing your attitude to become rich. Use it every day of your life write as much as you can, just like: I read books for at least 1 to 3 hours a day: I listen to audio podcast everyday: I attend seminar or take courses.

3. Whatever money you have, begin to manage it now. Do not wait another day, even if you only have a peso. Manage that peso. Take 25 cents and put it into your play jar. This single action will send a message to the world that you are ready for more money. If you can make more, manage more.

4. Write an affirmation and read it every day before you sleep. When you wake up in the morning, be thankful with the amount that you achieve every month. Same as: I am so happy and grateful that I am now earning 100,000 pesos per month. You decide how much money you want to achieve, and date when you want to get this. Repeat it ten (10) times. After that, close your eyes and imagine that you receive this amount of money, whether it's your bank or what you want to put in. Picture the life you want to have and the lifestyle you want; home; car; business that you want to perform. Place it on your pillow or wherever you want to place it close to your head before you fall asleep. Take action immediately on how you can get this.

5. Practice meditation every day for at least 30 minutes.

6. Exercise for at least 30 minutes and eat healthy food.

7. Open your Financial Freedom Bank account. Put 10% of your income and also the penny you save in the jar (after taxed) into this account. That money will never be spent but will be invested to generate passive income.

8. Bend your right arm in front of you and make a fist in your hand and say this:

I will become rich!

One more time.

I will become rich!

One more time.

I will become rich!

say it again and again.

Live like a rich

Bad habits aren't good

I started using cigarettes and alcohol when I was 12 years old under the influence of my neighbors. Until I reach the age of 25, every day I can consume almost 1 pack of cigarettes; 20 pieces of stick per pack. It costs 5 pesos per stick of Marlboro. Suppose I started smoking when I was 12, so I consume 20 pieces a day. Those costs 100 pesos per day, times 7 days that costs 700 per week. I consume 140 sticks per week, so it's 2,800 pesos multiplied by the number of sticks per month. I consume 560 sticks in 1 month which costs 16,800 pesos. Therefore, in a year, I consume 6,720 sticks of cigarettes which costs 36,000 pesos. I can almost buy a brand-new camera out of this amount for my vlog. I started smoking when I was 12 years old till I was 25 years old. For almost 13 years I have been using cigarettes multiplied by 83,360 per stick. In this year, this equates to 468,000 pesos per stick in 12 years until I turn 25. I can almost buy a house and lot on that amount. If this total amount is saved for 13 years each month in my stock market with 12% interest rate, and I keep it until I get to the age of 30. My total investment for today is 2,097,973.27 million pesos; I am a millionaire at the moment.

Not only that, but the price of cigarettes is going up each year. The inflation rate is always increasing their value. The cigarettes value today is 10 pesos per stick in 2021. If 10 pesos per day for today, and you do not consume it prior to the year 2041, you save 1,440,000 million pesos for 20 years per stick of cigarettes. Let's say you start placing it on the stock market today, 2021. Regularly, each month, you put it in stock for your cigarettes consume with a total of 5,600 pesos per month for 1 pack per day. After 20 years, your total amount of investment is 5,422,955.03 million pesos for the year 2041 with the interest rate of 12%.

So, you see, I waste all the money on my bad habits every day and not just a cigarette, but alcohol. Let's count the cost of alcohol, right now. When I started using alcohol at 12 years old, I can consume 2 bottles of 1 litre of red horse every day. The value of red horse at that time is 80 pesos per bottle. I consume 2 bottles a day equals to 160 pesos per day. In one week, I drink 14 bottles multiplied by 80 pesos per bottle, which gives us 1,120 pesos per week. In one month, I consume 56 bottles multiply by 80 pesos. This equals to 4,480 pesos per month. I consume 648 bottles per year times 80 pesos per bottle, its 51,840 pesos in only one year. Imagine, I can almost buy a brand-new iPhone 12 out of this quantity.

Let us count 12 years to 25 years consuming, 648 bottles times 13 years, which make a total of 8,424 bottles. In almost 13 years of drinking alcohol multiplied by 80 pesos, the total amount I consume is 673,920 pesos, I can build too many apartments on that amount.

If I combine the total cost of cigarettes with alcohol for 13 years: 468,000 plus 673,920, for a total of 1,141,920 million pesos. I was able to retire on that amount. If put it all on the stock market, how much is my overall investment? Its 8,779,712.27 MILLION PESOS!

You see, I waste all the money on the bad habits. And other than that, it's not only the pain in your pocket, but also its pain in your health. Because for almost consuming 13 years for my bad habits I got so many sicknesses, I experienced.

Study shows that, there is a significantly higher rate of suicide among people who abuse alcohol and/or drugs. Alcohol is involved in an estimated 30% of suicides. Alcohol causes depressed mood, lowers inhibitions, and impairs judgment, any or all of which may set up vulnerable people to act on suicidal plans.

I've seen a lot of people hanging out on the street on every corner, when they get drunk, they want to get in trouble. Sometimes they're off their minds and you can't control them because they're sober. I know some people, they're arrogant. They're always right. They think they know what they're doing, and a lot of them live in poverty. All they want in their lives is to get drunk and spend whatever they get for their bad habits. It's so hard to manage sober people because they're godly. They think they know everything about life. They are always wasting the money they will never get. That is why they remain poor and broke, because they cannot save their money. All they want to do is to enjoy, but the truth is, they're not having fun. They're useless. They have nothing to contribute to the world.

Powerful Advice

Friends, quit your bad habits as soon as possible since you cannot save if you stay with that. Every day you're consuming for nothing. How do you benefit from it? Other than the fact that it's unhealthy, you'll die early if you don't stop this habit. Remember, you only live once and you exchange your life for that? Our lives are God's most precious gift, use them well. Don't waste your life for consuming that thing. We have many big dreams; we want to live in this world forever. I feel a lot of regret for myself by consuming things that I could not benefit from. I'm wasting all the money I have. I don't save it for the future. I always think of enjoying. But the truth is, I never like this thing, because if I enjoy my bad habit, I don't regret it now.

It's time to change. It's never too late to quit. But it's too late, if you'll die early. You may not grow old with your habits, for you will die early.

> *"The wise man saves for the future. But the foolish man spends whatever he gets."*
>
> —*Proverbs 21:20*

Your bad habit friends are not your true friend

I have a lot of friends who only visit me if they need something. But if I need them, it's as if they are invisible, I don't even find them on social media. Do you experience that you are defeated in your life, and you need help from someone but no one helps you? It hurts, right?

I found out many times that if I looked for help for my friends, it was as if I was not known. But if they seek help for me, I respond directly.

I have learned this lesson that it is better to live alone in this world, because the one person who can help you is 'you'. I realize that when I have something that I have a lot of friends who care about. Every time I had a birthday party, I invited them all. Thus, I never attended their birthday even once. If my birthday is near, they are waiting for my celebration. Since they know that I spend my birthday for them, yet I never heard them say they invited me.

I once knew the day of the festival in the hometown of my friend, a friend of mine invited me to go to their place. But when we got there, she said, "Why are you here? You're not invited." I expected her to invite me, but when we went inside, that's all I heard. After that, I never went back to their house. However, I still invited her if I had an occasion.

I realize that whenever I was down, my only ally was myself. That's why I've never seen my friends anymore, because the truth is I've never had a good friend. If they're my friends, they're here whenever I need a hand. They're there whenever I have a problem, they're there whenever I fall down. But every time I had a problem, it was just me who could see me.

I have a lot of money before and I spend it all for my friends. Every time we hang out; every time we go to the club; out of town; going to another place where we can chill out; I spend all my money to them. Buy some beers, or grab some food, I'm the only one who spend it all. I thought I was happy with them but when I realized I was wasting so much money on somebody that I couldn't benefit from it. Whenever I had no money, I had no friends. I don't see them anymore. It hurts, isn't it? But that is the truth.

Powerful Advice

Friends, real friends can never let you go whether you have a problem or not. They are there to support you. A true friend is not based on money. It's based on trust, feelings, and love. If your friends right now who can benefit you only for your bad habits, I'm sorry to say this but, they're not your true friend. A real friend can't ever let you go, even when he can. If they really love you, they accept you for who you are, even if you have money or not.

Time is Running Out!

Did you know that
in 1 second, we have 1,000 milliseconds
in 60 seconds, we have one minute
in 60 minutes, we have an hour
in 24 hours, we have a day
in 7 days, we have a week
in 28-31 days, we have a month

in 365 or 366 days, we have a year

in 12 months, we have a year

in 10 years, we have a decade

In 100 years, one century

In 1,000 years, one millennium

When I was a kid, I used to play online games in the internet café. Sometimes I don't go to school, I cut classes because I just want to go to an internet café. I'm not like the other kids who focus only on studying; I don't read books. Unlike other students at the school who have personal tutor in their study; they also enroll in private school. Me, I don't care about my studies, As I have no father to guide me where I want to go. I don't have anybody to teach me the right thing to do, because my mom is always busy with her job. She never had time for me. I may have an older brother, but we're incompatible. We don't like each other until now when we get older.

When I was a teen, I spent all my time dancing. I love dancing when I was in my teens and I join a dance group. I was very passionate about in music, so I didn't have time to study. I've never read books since then. But I don't get paid for my fashion; it wasn't an advantage to me. Although I like music, I don't make money. I never earn money for that. Even in college, I waste my time and effort for something that did not benefit me. Perhaps that's why I haven't grown up. I didn't earn, because since then I never learn how to make money. I exchange my time for nothing. I never think about helping my mom to earn. I just enjoying myself. I was so selfish.

Until the time when I was in Manila, I started working and reading books. I realize this when I use all my time reading books and earning money. How far I can go right now? I did not realize that in order for you to multiply your money, you need to multiply your time. You need to read books. You need to use your time by making money. I have so much time that I have to work for studies. Either way, I'm wasting it all. I'm just using it for something I wouldn't be able to benefit from.

I have noticed for the poor that they always play mobile games. Every time I walk down the street, I thought they were wasting their time for nothing. What are the benefits that they get for playing mobile games? I also used to play before when I was an employee, yet now I realize every second that I waste playing online games is having a big impact on me. Knowing what I learned when playing mobile games? How do I benefit from that? Is your IQ increasing when you're playing? Is your income increasing or is it going to be exhausting?

You are always confused and you complain of the reasons why you remain broke and poor. But you still give more importance to mobile games. You have no right to complain, because in the beginning, it is your fault that you remain poor.

Think of it, it's just 24 hours a day, and in that 24 hours you need to sleep, work, eat and everything that you personally. How can you divide your time? Do you think you can live forever in this world? Do you think you will live 200 years? Do you still have an energy when you get older? Do you still work when you grow old? Do you still have money when we don't have time?

Powerful Advice

Friends, never waste your time. Use it well, because we don't know when was our time. I've already wasted too much time before. If I use it for reading books and improving myself, I am more than a wise person for today. Reason why entrepreneurs hire more employees so they can use their time for others. We only got 24 hours a day; that wasn't enough for them. Then they need to multiply them by using another people's time.

"The only difference between the rich and the poor person is what they do in their spare time. Free time is more and more precious."

—*Robert Kiyosaki*

The early bird catches the worm.

According to research at Harvard University, early birds are more proactive—and thus more productive and efficient. Researchers at Drexel University have discovered that early birds have lower body mass index (BMI) than night owls. The research also found that those who are in place earlier usually show happier moods, lower depression level, and higher motivation. A Finnish study even shown that those who stayed up later were eventually more likely to end up abusing alcohol and tobacco, sometimes even taking anti-depressants.

The reason for this may very well be the increase in

the amount of communication that occurs after the morning passes. When more people are awake, we all remain as interconnected as we are in today's technology-driven—social media world. We are more likely want to participate in social events, talk with others, or just scroll through our news feeds looking for the next update.

So, if you're an early riser, consider yourself lucky. You're already getting a head start to your day; the success you have worked so hard to achieve, in both your work and your life.

"I am the vine: You are the branches. If you remain in me and in you, you will bear much fruit. Apart from me you can do nothing."

—*John 15:5*

Why is so hard to live in a poverty area?

Poverty area is the nosiest place on earth. Apart from too many people who live there, the house is merging on each other. If you're the kind of person like me who wants to get some peace and concentrate on his work; you cannot survive in the poverty area. In 24/7 there are too many people around the street; trolling around even it was already midnight. If you want to have peace and concentrate your work, you need to transfer in the sub-division area. Therefore, it is better to become rich so that you can choose to live where you want. It is so hard if you are distracted by your work, especially when you are reading books. You can't comprehend what you're reading because your mind was distracted. I am that kind of person every time I have something to do. I am easily distracted by the noise around my neighbors at my apartment. That's why I can't survive in poverty, because I'm a type of person who loves reading. Aside from it, it is impossible to please those who live in poverty area, for you shall become evil if you please them. Hindi mo madadaan sa pakiusap ang taong mahirap. All they want is violence.

We are not able to do anything because our government is almost the same. The fact is that, even if you're born poor, if you're determined to become rich, you must find ways to live your life better. Sometimes it is not due to the government. It's our fault because we accept our situation just like that. We cannot find ways to live a better life. Even if you live in the poorest country on earth, if you determine to become rich, you will become rich. People always blame the government for their situation, but they haven't done a thing in their lives. They only know that it is to complain to government. Even though you think you should do something, you will never change the government. Anything you can do rather than change the government. You have to change yourself instead. No matter how much the government changes, but if you don't change, nothing will happen to your lives.

That is why poor people do not grow up, because they are only waiting for government help. You cannot please everyone in this world, because they have their own lives too. They have also a family just like you. Instead of begging others, we must be responsible for ourselves.

"You may be the poorest man on the continent, and deeply in dept.

You may have neither friend, influence, resources. But if you begin to do things in this way, you must infallibly begin to get rich. No matter how poor you may be, if you begin to do things in a certain way you will begin to get rich."

—*Wallace D. Wattles*

Rich Mindset Activity Action Exercise

1. Write down the five (5) or more bad habits that you have right now, and make the decision to quit. If it's hard to quit smoking, you minimize it until you totally get out from your habits. Make a daily habit just like: I'm smoking 5 sticks today: I will smoke 3 sticks tomorrow: I smoked 1 stick the other day. Till it becomes your habit to stop and focus on your goals. Remember that saving is impossible if you keep your bad habits.

2. Write down the five (5) or more new habits that you want to start now by changing your life, as does: I'm starting to save money to invest: I'll set aside my money for the bad habit of my savings: I will invest all the money that I save.

3. List the five (5) or more things you want to eliminate that might make you waste your time each day. And focus on the things that you can benefit.

4. Make a time management and daily schedule.

Time	Activity
6:00 am - 6:30 am	Wake-up in the morning.
6:30 am - 7:00 am	Meditate
7:00 am	Exercise

Make your own preferred schedule and constantly work on it daily.

5. Write down the five (5) ways and why you want to escape into poverty. Start living where you want to live in comfort.

6. Bend your arm straight in front of you and make a fist in your hand and say this:

I will become rich!

One more time.

I will become rich!

One more time.

I will become rich!

say it again and again.

Investments strategy of the rich

The Secret of the Rich

"Someone is sitting in the shades today, because someone planted it a long time ago."

—*Warren Buffet*

Investment is one of the secrets to rich people in terms of earning more money. Rich people acquired assets through investment. They always make passive income through stock market, cryptocurrency, mutual funds, real state and more. Tell me a billionaire who has no investment. All the billionaires in the world make profit through investments. Hence, keep this in mind before you start investing to avoid repentance: The higher the interest, the higher the risk.

The investment is like a seed, if you put your money in the bank, it means a dead money. If you plant the seed on the investment, that creates income. The seeds will grow for a period of time, since the money in the bank it depreciates their value every year. The inflation rate changes every year. It's not about how much money you save; it's about how much money you grow.

Why the bank gets so rich?

The secret of the bank why they're so rich is because you still transact there. As an example, you deposit your money in the bank. For every amount you deposit in the bank, they will give you a 1% interest rate per annum after taxes. In other words, you are the ones that need help with your loan. Let's say you want to loan a house. You make a loan to the bank where you put your money. The bank lets loan for you with the interest rate of 6-8% interest rate per year. If you decide to build a business, and you lend it to the bank, the interest rate per annum is 12-15% interest rate.

For credit card, if you want to get a credit card and the bank allows you to lend back; it will loan you at the interest rate of 3-5% per month (42% per year). In other words, if you put money just to save in the bank, they will give you the 1% interest rate. This will charge you 6% to 42% on every loan you make. The bank makes profits from every money you save, and every loan you make. First and foremost, that is your money. Money in the bank is high risk, due to inflation and increased taxes caused by banks printing money. If the bank tells you that your interest rate is 8% per annum, is that true? I've found that it's not about learning to read numbers.

The secret of the rich, they will invest your money and let it grow. Every transaction you do for them, they make more money on you.

Don't wait to buy a real estate, buy a real estate and wait.

When I started earning money during the pandemic, I save all my money in the bank. After months of selling, I can save thousands of pesos; all of my monthly income goes to the bank. I noticed that in every deposit at the bank, there wasn't any growth; it was almost the same money. I put in the previous amount that I deposited last month. Whenever I buy goods on the market, the price is always depreciating their value. Those five pesos sili (chili pepper) I bought yesterday become 20 pesos. I thought that if I left my money in the bank after a year or five, nothing would happen with my money. I was going bankrupt, because the value of goods in the market is always depreciating. The inflation rate is always increasing. Inflation for today during the year October 2021 is 5%. The bank's interest rates each year is only below 1%. If you have plans to save 100,000 pesos at the bank to purchase a new car in the future. Maybe in the future you can only buy a tire for your 100,000 pesos. It is better to buy it now, while not increasing inflation more.

I look for properties in Bulacan. I try house and lot, but it's too expensive. It was handled by PAG-IBIG and it is worth 1,5 million pesos. I went to PAG-IBIG office to inquire their properties. However, the problem is that I'm not capable of buying a property through PAG-IBIG. My savings at PAG-IBIG is only 7 months, when I began working as a service crew until I was laid off on my job. I will not put more money there every month. I have lost my job. The necessary funds of PAG-IBIG are at least 9 months of savings. There are so many documents I could work before being able to buy a property via PAG-IBIG.

Therefore, I try to look at the properties via online. I join Facebook group for the house and lot. I found an agent who's trying to sell his land in Bulacan. I went there and by the grace of God I bought it for 8,000 pesos per square meter; I bought 40 square meters. The place is subdivision type and it's already developed. Many people already live there. Monthly I put 4,000 pesos on this land with an interest rate of 0%. Until I complete the square meter of 40 by the total amount. After I pay for the remainder of this land, I will sell it at a higher price.

Imagine if I just let the bank handle my money. After five years, do you think this will increase the value of my money each month I make a deposit? It is better to buy a property now and wait for the next few years; sell it at a higher price. As I said before, the land will not depreciate their value. It always increases the value. The higher the demand, the higher the value. The more population we have, the more I can sell it at a higher price.

If you are looking for a long-term investment, land property is good. Thus, if you want to have a passive income every month, rental property is the best choice. Despite that it is cost much; need to have a big capital and perfect location. The interesting thing about a land property is that you can inherit it on your children. If you want, you can live in it forever by building a home. However, if you decide to live in your property, it is no longer an investment; you call it now a liability. Always remember this, a house you live has never been an asset. Governments tax you even if you own them.

Take note! Before you buy a property make sure you read all the documents and background of the company. Ensure that the developer is good. There are properties that are affordable, but money that is not returned to their clients. Choose developer that have proven record themselves when it comes to product development, entitled and documentation, after-sales service. Don't just buy, you must also be a truly wise state investor. One good thing about the pandemic today is that the real estate market is falling down; you can buy affordable unit. By the way, find the right location that can suit your budget and check out. Consider prospective market value potential in this area, so you're making the right decision for yourself.

The End of the Industrial Age and the Start of the Information Age.

Did you know that in 1492, the voyage of Columbus marked the start of the industrial age? It was at the end of 1989 that the Berlin Wall was destroyed as a communist and the information age began.

Be careful with the markets.

Some poor people hop into an employee to

investors so they have a security. Either way, they don't even know that the investment is for risk-takers. There are people who believe that if they invest today, tomorrow, their money will be doubled. That's the most dangerous decision you made. Invest what you just want to lose.

When it comes to investing, you must be prepared for what will happen in the marketplace. If the purpose of your investment is for your wedding, I am certain that tomorrow your wife will not be with you anymore. Investment is not guaranteed. You can't predict the market when it's going to go up; it's very complicated. You can't predict if you can earn or not. Still, there are mathematicians and analysts who do studies to predict the market, and they were the expert.

Let's say, you have a wedding day in 6 months. Before marriage, you have capital worth 500,000 pesos. You are not content with your capital, because you want a grand wedding. You want to hire a famous photographer; have a concert with Eraserheads; would like to have a celebrity to attend at your wedding. So, you need a huge capital on this event. Therefore, you decided to invest in the stock market. You expect the 500,000 pesos to turn into millions.

You're so excited about your wedding; you already got a dress for your bride; rent a luxury car to surprise your wife that you are so fancy. You take a risk, because your money is not enough for your wedding. You assume that your 500,000 pesos will turn into millions. Thus, after 6 months the market drops to -50%; even in the first day the market may have dropped dramatically

50%. Your 500,000 pesos, after six months, becomes 250,000 pesos. The grand wedding that you promise has been cancelled. The wedding was 100% secure on the exact day of the event, now due to your bad decisions, your wife will no longer be with you.

Start Investing in Stock Market

Some people get scammed due to a lack of financial education in schools. Most people blindly give their money to people they regard as financial experts such as: bankers, financial planner, and stockbrokers. However, many of them are not real investors. Most of them are employed for a pay check, or a freelance financial consultant working for fees and commissions. These experts cannot afford to stop working simply because they do not have any investment at their disposal.

> *"Wall street is the only place that people ride in a Rolls Royce; to get advice from those who take the subway."*
>
> —*Warren Buffet*

How to Earn in the Stock Market?

There are two ways to earn in stock market

1. Capital Appreciation
2. Dividends

CAPITAL APPRECIATION
(Buy Low, Sell High)

When you buy shares in a company, the stock price increases relative to the initial price. For example, let's say you bought Ayala Land (ALI) shares for 40 pesos per stock and kept them for 3 months. As you look at your stocks, you see that every share is now worth 44 peaks; this increase is what you call Capital Appreciation.

DIVIDENDS

There are two types of dividends.

1. Cash Dividends ➢ These are determined by the earnings of the company. The concept of cash dividends is that if the company receives more cash than it needs to expand, it can choose to reward its shareholders by paying dividends.

2. Stock Dividends ➢ They are normally given when the company wants to reward their investors without paying for it. The stock dividend work if the Board Director has approved the number of shares given to shareholders as stock dividends you may receive.

What Is Cryptocurrency?

A cryptocurrency is a digital or virtual currency that is protected by cryptography, which makes counterfeiting or double spending almost impossible. Many cryptocurrencies are decentralized networks that rely on blockchain technology: a distributed ledger enforced by a disparate network of computers.

Why you should invest in Crypto Currency?

The blockchain technology that underpins Bitcoin and other cryptocurrencies has been hailed as a potential game changer for a large number of industries. From shipment and supply chains to banking and healthcare services. By eliminating intermediaries and trusted actors from computer networks, distributed ledgers can facilitate new types of economic activities that were previously unavailable.

This potential makes an investment appealing to those who believe in the future of digital currencies. For those who believe in this promise, investing in cryptocurrency is a way to earn high returns while sustaining the future of technology.

Another common reason for investing in cryptocurrency is the desire for a reliable and long-term store value. In contrast to fiat money, most cryptocurrencies have a limited supply, capped by mathematical algorithms. This makes it impossible for a political body or government agency to dilute their value through inflation.

Potential or Speculation?

While many advocates believe that digital currencies may become a part of everyday life, the cryptocurrency market is currently dominated by speculative trading. Studies of blockchain activity show that trade continues to be the most widespread use for cryptocurrencies; account for far more economic activity than ordinary trades and purchases. Skeptical cryptocurrency, including Warren Buffett, Bill Gates, and JPMorgan CEO Jamie Dimon have all cautioned against a potential cryptocurrency bubble.

Not all wise man had college degrees.

Many people had a college degree; have a good education.

They had skills in arithmetic, trigonometry, chemistry, physics, French, English literature: had many more responsibilities. Somehow, most successful people went off to school like: Thomas Edison (founder of general electric), Henry Ford (founder of Ford motor Co.), Bill gates (founder of Microsoft), Steve Jobs (founder of Apple), Ralph Lauren (founder of POLO), Elon Musk (founder of Space X and Tesla), Mark Zuckerberg (founder of Facebook). They acquired assets and investments.

The school is not teaching you about how to be financial freedom. That's why I don't focus on my study. When I went to school, I spent my time in network marketing and sales. Since, I know the school doesn't teach me to make more money.

Get involved in Network Marketing

Network marketing is one of the recommendations I make when you start selling products. There is no need to innovate your product; just make sure the company is good. When I was recruited for a network marketing before, I study the company first. I'm researching their products. Network marketing is also one of the best personal franchises when you begin to build a business. For just 3000 pesos depending on the company's offer, you can start selling products and expand your network. Many advisors and distributors in the network marketing they became successful because of their hard work. Just like in any other form of a business, there's always a rejection; how not being affected by what other people say, and how to lead people.

There's nothing wrong with network marketing just ensuring that their products are good. The system builds leadership to guide people on how to grow. I had met many people who were also diligently successful managed for their network marketing business. I also met people who are scammed into network marketing by allowing others to manipulate their money.

There are some people who are successful in network marketing, but after a few years they will be bankrupt. Their lifestyle was increasing, and they want to look rich. In network marketing, they don't teach you about managing your money. They do not teach you the basics of financial literacy. All they focus on are products and services. Even though your income is much more, if you don't have an idea about finances, it will be exhausted and worse, you will get into debts. It is better to start small so whenever you failed you can overcome quickly.

However, the good thing about network marketing is that it provides people with the ability to build passive income. They must support them as they learn to become investors. If you can handle the finances, marketing, and investments, there's nothing wrong with that. Remember, it's better to be on sales than in day to day job.

How to Avoid Scam?

If someone offers you a low interest rate if it's too good to be true, it definitely isn't true. Don't believe in that investment, since real investment takes time. It takes a lot of years to grow. Before you get your return, do not send any amount of money in least than 30 or 60 days. Moreover, do not believe in the guarantee. In all investments, there is no guarantee; even in the traditional business there's no guaranteed. How much more in investment? There's always a risk.

If someone's offer you with zero risk, do not believe in that. Scammers know that people are prepared not to take risks. But I'm telling you that if that's still what you think, you're still getting into a scam. Always remember that the higher the interest, the higher the risk. If they use high-pressure selling pitch like: It's a limited edition. Get yours now! Don't believe in that, because they always use your F.O.M.O (fear of missing out). Sometimes, they offer you a freebie in exchange for investment. It's better to be safe, critical and vigilant.

Read all the documents first. Don't hesitate to ask questions; ask someone who knows it better. You can send me an email on my social media. I can guide you in the right way.

If you fail to get 101% of your question, that's total scam. Don't be too excited. Control your emotions. Control your money. Don't immediately send someone online or otherwise. Don't sign right away unless you're sure. Do not allow the F.O.M.O to dictate your emotions. Talk to a third-party consultant such as lawyer, an accountant and a financial advisor like myself. That could be anyone you can trust. Someone who has enough knowledge when it comes to money and give you an advice on your plan.

Investors generate money through their investment while employees are holding jobs and working for a company.

For almost 1 year of being an employee as a service crew, I never enjoy my work. There are times when I don't feel comfortable getting to work. I always tell my ex-girlfriend that I wasn't so happy about what I was doing at the moment. Perhaps I never forget what the network marketing thought me. It's always on my head; it's spinning whenever I do my job. My ex-girlfriend response, "Just bear with it as long as you have a job."

However, in my heart there is one thing I want to achieve. Every time I get to work, I lose interest, I don't care what my co-workers told me. I've got another world. I can't relate to them. Whenever they laughed and talked about our work, I could not understand what they were saying. It's like I'm on the wrong side of the world. I didn't appreciate what they're doing. I feel so stressed and uninterested every time I do my job. Maybe I'm unhappy with my work.

And until the pandemic comes in I was fired on my job. After almost three months of lockdown, the good thing is that I have savings for my previous job. My savings are about setting up my own small business. Ever since, I got a plan to start my own small business. Which is why I save 30% of my salary. Unfortunately, all my savings have been spent on rent and food so I can survive the pandemic. My plan is gone because I spent it all for my needs. Thus, on the first day of GCQ (General Community Quarantine) I buy face shield online and sell it around Monumento in Caloocan. Therefore, that was the first day of my journey to becoming an entrepreneur.

Security over Freedom

Whenever I hear the word "security" coming out of my head, I remember my big brother. He has worked as a call center agent for almost 10 years. I tried to convince him in sales when I was in a network marketing, yet he always refuses me. He said, "You're wasting your time for that, why don't you focus on your study?" mom was spending so much on your study; she was throwing it away because of what you're doing right now

Actually, his right because I exchange my education

in sales without making any profit; I never had a downline. If my friends and relatives trust me and join me in network marketing, maybe I'm rich right now. They also got rich, but no one trusted me. No one will join me. Instead, criticism is their first priority. That's why my friends will never grow up. They only knew is how to criticize me. All they want is to pull me down; by talking of my bad personality. Sometimes God keeps people away from you, because he heard a conversation that you didn't.

The saddest truth is, your friends are there if you got something you can benefit from them. However, when it comes to trust, they will never trust you especially when it comes to opportunities. If they know about you're in the network marketing, they don't want to see you anymore. You're like a monster who'll make them afraid. That is why they had many dreams that could not be fulfilled, because we do not support each other. Instead, we're prepared to criticize. If we do not support and help each other, nothing will happen in our lives.

That's why some people are afraid of fulfilling their dreams again, because they failed once. Nothing is going to come forward, since we're not going to help. Our economy will never change considering that people are so rejected and subjected to discrimination. This is the result of strays for some people, and worst, they will end up by taken drugs; just like what happen to me before. Unsuccessful people still drag you down. All they want is for you to never succeed in life. Even though they had so many things in life, all they want is not to lose. Only anger prevails them and hatred.

We live in this world with so much hatred. We let us not forget the war which took place in the past. This is already 2021, and our population was growing. Tomorrow we will live in space, but hatred still prevails us. We have come here to expand our race; to multiply around the universe. Humans are expanding, but they are not growing. They are still immature.

If my friends and relatives support me in my dreams, I can graduate in college without any regret. I can pay my tuition without the help of my mother. Instead, I end up using drugs, because no one supports me in my sales (which is my dream). But it's never too late to do it again, which is why I'm back to selling now. I'm selling balut in the street for a fresh start; that's the beginning of my entrepreneurship.

Why poor people broke once they get old?

My father was an educated man who graduated from law school. Before he died (I was five years of age), he gave so much thought to my brother in his study. According to him, when my brother went to kindergarten, he was an honor student.

My father was a smart person, but he failed in his family. He is a professor in college at the university. When he retires, he ends up at the local barber shop in Cebu. He had little benefit from his teaching career; without savings. This is why we always move from one house to another with no fixed address. He died without a thing to establish for his children. This is why we suffer after his death. All the materials and heir was taken from us. Which is why my mother was the only one who solved the problem. My father had nothing to do with his kids before he died. He has a good education with a bachelor's degree, but lack of knowledge about retirement funds and life insurance. He is proud of his diploma, but has nothing to do with his family for the future. He is still looking for job security for his retirement; hoping the government can secure his family's future. And because he focused on his education, his family was transferred repeatedly to another location with no permanent home. He should be grateful that my grandfather (my mother's father), provided us a great deal to build a new home in the province. Without my grandfather's help, we sleep in the street after he's dead.

You should be on Sales

Me and my brother are alike. He gives up his education for benefits and I give up my education for freedom. I was very passionate about in sales. If I do well in sales before, I also do well in my studies. Since I can provide all my tuition. Sadly, I was surrounded by a poor people, whom all they want is to hate me. All they know about their lives is that they hate me, criticize me, even if I don't do anything with them. All they see about me is how unpleasant I am, they're not focusing on themselves. They just look at other people's lives.

My brother used to work in a call center. When he was 18 years old, he stopped studying to start working as a call center agent in Cebu. While I continue to study when I was in network marketing; even though I did not earn much. I have no downlines, I've never had one. The nuggets and wisdom every day in the seminar that I learn for nearly years participating in network marketing, is the beginning of my learning in entrepreneurship; still existing today. Despite that I'm wasting all my mother's money, because I'm focused on selling. I am still happy being an entrepreneur. I like talking to people. I love negotiating. This is the life I want to live; to have more freedom when I grow up. I never think about the present, I always think about the future.

How do you define benefits?

When I hear the word 'benefits', it's more like people who always like some extra rewards—some extra compensation insured like health insurance or a retirement plan. My brother is always looking for security. He wants the government to ensure that his family has a future. He always expects governments in return. If you ask him about opportunities, he always say that he's not interested in money. For him security is more important than money, it is fear that dictates his emotion. That's why he avoids taken risks.

But for me, I want to find out more about technical skills such as: financial statements, marketing, sales, accounting, management, production, negotiation, and more. Reason why I've always failed on every semester. I choose to have technical business skills. I choose to listen to the entrepreneurs' speech at the seminar rather than listening to my college teacher. I want to have the ability to lead people.

Leadership is one of my skills when it comes to managing people, because in every organization you have to be a leader to manage it.

> *"The rise and fall of every organization is leadership."*
> —*John Maxwell*

Don't depend on the government's benefits.

When my brother leaves on vacation, his income stops as well. As he uses time to work for his income. If my brother is sick and leaves his job for him to stay in the hospital to recover; his income stops working as well. During which time my brother stops working for months and years, his income also stops. However, his daily expenses never stop.

So, I ask you one question: What do you think my brother provides to the government for his family when he stops working? The answer is: just medical insurance and retirement plan. Do you think that the retirement plan can provide their children during their studies? Not really because, apart from the tuition of his children, he also provided his family with a mortgage, food, and other necessities.

This is the thing, does your money work for you and generate ongoing income for you? If not, you are now dependent on government policy. If governments tell you that your funds no longer exist, since all the funds are no longer available. (Just like what happened to the

PhilHealth recently; the 15 billion pesos scammed from their corruption.) Do you think the government can give you 100% for your retirement?

People are so desperate for retirement and waiting years to know if they will get their money back. They do not even realize that the government has taken advantage of their security funds. They are working so hard to get a higher tax rate than investors. But the investors are getting richer and making millions with little or no tax.

Investors are working less, earning more and paying less taxes, but employees are working more with the tax deducted from their wages.

We are now in the Information Age, forget about Industrial Age.

Poor people are always avoid taking risk. They do not like the idea of managing money relative to their hard-earned money, and possibly not coming back. They are very careful with their money, regardless of how much they might earn back. Which is why they choosing to put all their money into the bank so they wouldn't lose it. And if your company announced that they will no longer be responsible for your retirements for years, you are now investing responsibly into your own retirement plan.

We also have to be wiser investors to prepare for the information age; to know what will happen to our economy. Do not rely only on your job security. We must also focus on our own financial security. Learn to take risks and be market conscious for both ups and downs.

It is the industrial age which teaches them to go to school; to find a stable job, and to be safe. That is the concept of people born in 1930. Today, everybody must know how to invest, but investing has never been taught in school. As you know, in the United States, social security is expected to be bankrupt by 2037. Medical care insurance is bankrupt by 2017. The industrial age is history and we have to prepare for the possibilities of the information age. The age of the industry is the benefit of a pension plan signified by the guarantee of the company to you. We must be responsible for ourselves right now, and learn how to take calculated risk.

"You can't study to be an entrepreneur.

Sometimes, you just have to jump." —Barbara Corcoran

It's not how much money you have, but how much money you grow.

At the age of 18, I went to college. My weekly allowance is 2,000 pesos. It only lasts three days while spending time at a club, partying with my dormmates, and buying brand shirts. After that, I call my mother for an extra 2,000 pesos, then I spend it again. Therefore, my monthly allowance was estimated at 24,000 pesos a month. Imagine if I save my 50% weekly allowance for investment. It is 3,000 times 4 which makes 12,000. I could have saved 12,000 pesos for my investment per month. If I save it for annual, so we have 144,000 pesos. I can almost buy a lot in Bulacan on that amount. If I invested it every month in the stock market, and invested it regularly until I quit studying at the age of 25, within 18 to 25 years (8 years on studying at the college), so my overall investment was 1,983,694.51 million pesos. If I keep invested it till I reach my age of 30 today, my investment for today is 4,520,534.75 million pesos.

Unfortunately, my money now is only 20 pesos. How do I grow on that amount? If only I could turn back in time, I could be a millionaire. I used to eat McDonald's in Ayala every day, but now I eat canned sardines in my boarding house. I used to wear brand tribal shirts every day, but now I've been content to use regular shirts with the teddy bear printed in front. Before I went to the club partying with my dormmates, but now I used to stay at home drinking 3n1 coffee. Thinking how do I get that money back.

You see, I waste all the money that I had. If you have a YOLO mentality (you only live once) at the moment, now it's time for you to change it to YAGO (you all get old). The moment you realize your money is wasted on nothing, it's too late. When you're older, you'll figure out how to get that money back. I don't think about the future then, I still think it's enjoying for the present. As I get older, I realize how much money I used to waste; it's a big thing for me right now.

Learn to evaluate your money. Since, when the right time has come and you ran out of money; it is so hard to adopt when you have a lot of money.

Before I don't appreciate the big amount; I just want to spend it all. Now, 20 pesos is precious money to me. It's a lot of value to me now. Previously I do not appreciate the 2,000 pesos each week, but now I value the small amount of 20 pesos.

The advantage of a teenager at the moment is that he has more time to invest in the stock market because of the time horizon. The more time you have, the faster your money grows. If you are a teenager right now, and you plan to invest your 30% or 50% monthly allowance in the stock market. At 30 years old you will become a millionaire and financially free.

Rich Mindset Activity Action Exercise

1. Look for real estate broker online. Inquire them about the properties. Start purchase to invest in real estate. It is either condominiums, house and lot, or land.

2. Make an accordions envelope as much as you can. Put name in every envelope for savings. For example:

    Envelope 1   10% for Emergency Funds
    Envelope 2   30% for Real Estate
    Envelope 3   20% for Stock Market

You must have to put money on every envelope daily, weekly, or monthly according to your income.

3. Find an online broker and create a stock market account. Then, starting investing. It's either COL Financial, 2TradeAsia, first METROSEC, BPI Nomura, or whatever broker you preferred.

4. Change your focus to active income to passive income. List strategies you might use to generate income without working; either investment, or business. Begin research, and take action on these strategies.

5. If you want to start investing in

Cryptocurrencies, I suggest to open a Binance account. This is the only platform you can use to invest in NFTs, Mining, and other blockchain technology.

6. Bend your arm straight in front of you and make a fist in your hand and say this: I will become rich!

One more time.

I will become rich!

One more time.

I will become rich!

say it again and again.

You can't be rich by thinking poor.

Regardless of how ugly your past is, the importance is how beautiful your future

When I was young, I would meet different kinds of people on the street, because nobody has looked after me since I was a child. My brother hated me so much. I have no idea why he beat me every day. As a child, I'm not a resistance fighter when it comes to trouble. I don't know how to fight. I've been a coward ever since. Considering that my mother was too busy to work, she doesn't have time for me.

That means my brother and I were left at house. I've been afraid of him since my childhood. I've never liked my brother in my entire life because of what he's done to me in the past. I force myself to sleep in the street every day when I was a little boy. I don't want to come home, because my brother was in the house trying to kill me every day. It is then that I meet these two people in my life. I am not the other rich kids whose parents are very strict. They are still here, guiding them, caring for them, and giving love to their children. Nevertheless, no one has loved me since; even my neighbors have hated me since I was a toddler. It's so hard when you grow up with no father, because the people around you were oppression. Sometimes if something's missing from my neighbors, I will be the one who's been mistaken for a thief.

Which is why I preferred to sleep in the street to have peace. Even so, the street is more dangerous to sleep because you meet difficult people there. There are times when I sleep on the street someone stole my sleepers. Once I wake up, I don't have any sleepers. Often when I wake up, my body was full of scars on cigarettes. I always run into troubles on the street. Let me tell you right now, if your parents are both still alive, you're the luckiest person you think you are. If your parents love you so much, be grateful. Knowing that it's the hope of many children on the street like me before. I still think that if my dad's still alive, there's someone who defends me now. Sadly, he has already died. All I did was be with myself, loving myself and accepting myself for what I am; even though I have been born alone ever since. I am ever grateful that God gives me a precious life.

Due to what happened in my life from the past, all I want now is to become rich. If I remain poor, my life is not going to change. All I want now is to get rich, because remaining poor and broke, no one will treat you right. Poverty will not give you happiness, you will only suffer oppression. Some say, "I was born poor and I shall die poor." But to me, "I was born poor, but I shall die rich!"

From my past experiences, I use it to grow stronger right now. Instead of accepting what I've been, I'm using it to become more valuable today. If you retain your position before, there is no change for you. You're the same person that you were in the past.

If you think your situation is worse right now, I'm in a worse position than you know.

I haven't accepted myself as poor since. If you accept yourself as poor, no matter how ugly and evil your past is, you will live your life unhappy forever. Do not punish yourself because of what happened in the past. If God gives your life to have an abundance to make the best of it; cherished the moment as long as you are still alive. Money is not the most important aspect of life, but money affects everything that is important.

You do not need to be afraid if you want to become rich, as long as you will not do bad things. That way, if you get rich because you kill someone, you'll never be happy for the rest of your life. Though, if you use your wealth to build prosperity for others, you don't have to be afraid.

Wake up, and get real. Get your hands dirty and do your work honestly. The world does not owe you a living. This world is here before you were born. Therefore, work hard and help make the world a better place.

"Build a dream, and the dream will build you."
—Robert H. Schuller

You have a choice.
Make the right decision.

Some people are unhappy with their relationship. Many regrets and blame one another for their misfortune. But first of all, why are you two together when you blame each other?

I remember my brother who always tells me this: Jo find a girl that you really wanted, because my wife, I don't think I really like her. [I was so confused when he said that.] But as far as I'm concerned, why will you settle to a person you don't like?

Firstly, you already know that you don't like this person. Why you keep trying to be with someone you don't like? You owe your life; you can choose whoever you want to be with. There are many women out there, and you choose to settle for one girl you don't like. He is now married, and he has many regrets over his relationship.

> Did you know that survey says:
> In 2019, there were 16.3 new marriages for every 1,000 women aged 15. Over in the United States, down from 17.6 in 2009.

At the same time, the U.S. divorce rate fell from 9.7 new divorces per

1,000 women aged 15 (in

2009) up to 7.6 (in 2019).

This afternoon, I went to the Church and the Gospel speaks of

divorce. The priest said, "In the sixteenth century in England when the Church of England separated from the authority of a pope, and the Roman Catholic Church, Henry VIII's wish that his marriage be annulled in 1527. The legacy of the Roman Catholic heritage and establishment of the state church remained controversial for many years; still exists.

Before taking a vow to your spouse, and putting rings on her finger, make sure that your love for her is precious. You have to think twice about whether this person is the right person you wanted for the rest of your life, or you are just being replaced. Never think that you are not with anyone, and you are alone in your life. You know what, if that's the situation, I'd rather be on my own than be with the person that uncertainty. Marriage is so sacred. Before you say, in front of the altar, for sickness and in health, till death do as apart. Ensure that you sign it with care, not only in the Church, but also in heaven. Make sure this person is the only one you want. Even when you live in heaven, you will always be with them.

We are always abandoned one upon the other, but do you not think that Jesus Christ never abandoned us? How frequently have you abandoned God? How many times do you have a problem and you seek help from God? He always answers our prayers. Still, you didn't keep your promise to him.

The reason a toxic or unhealthy relationship exists is because it is uncertain. They don't even grow up on their individual lives. They don't have a choice between moving in with someone they don't really like. The only purpose of their lives is to get married. They did not see the perspective of their lives. They did not see a way to improve their lives. Don't force yourself to be with someone who is not sure; we are different sought on our lives. If you can't find the right person, focus on yourself. Just be with yourself, and love yourself. Stay single. Before you love others, you must first love yourself. For if you do not love yourself, you will not learn to love others. If you learn to love yourself, now is the time. God will provide you the right person that is destined to you. Enjoy your lifelong journey. Don't be so stressful about your relationship. You were born alone in this world; you'd have to die alone. How does a relationship help if you're not happy?

Why poor people are unhappy with their relationship?

This kind of people have no purpose in their lives, all they know is to have some comfort. If they find their way into life, they don't settle down like this. If they had a purpose in life, they concentrate on their passion and purpose. If you have an aim in your life, even if you live in this world alone, you are always happy without someone to comfort you. If you are satisfied with your goal, you do not need someone to guide you. You go your own way. You make your own destiny, you actually make something happen. Contrary to, if you are satisfied with your life right now and do not give time to seek out your goal., you shall live in this world of misery forever. The point is the one thing that would make us happy. You don't need somebody to be with, as long as you're happy with what you're doing. But if you seek anyone to comfort you, you will never be happy.

"Perseverance is stubbornness with a purpose."
—*Josh Shipp*

Focus on your grind and purpose.

Our purpose is our fundamental gift that dictates our hearts. We are not restless unless we carry out our mission in life. It's the reason you wake up every day, because of this passion you have right now. I tried something different but I failed. I tried to start a small business but I failed. I've tried working in the fast food chain and I've lost interest. But whenever I wrote something, my mind changed. I became someone else. I got a lot of information on my head. I guess it's God who put me in my heart, ever since I started writing a song. Unluckily, some people already find their purpose, but they do not care for it. They let their purpose flow away and ignore it.

You know that prior to your birth in this world, God placed each of us a destiny; in our hearts, and our minds; in the line of our soul. If you stay on that line, where you could find your way to get into your destiny, your life becomes much happier. If you cross this line, you fall in the river which is full of distraction, discouragement, low self-esteem, and envy. If you let it get into your emotion, you'll stay there forever.

It's never too late to start, even though you only have a few months left in this world. You can still fulfill your dreams. God has given you time. Somehow, if you don't work on them now, your destiny will be unrighteousness.

If you still breathe now, take some time to look over it. It is never too late to find the path that you wanted. God gives you time to make a difference. Don't focus on your comfort. Take time to find your goal. Keep grinding. Keep on dreaming. Keep climbing.

Keep yourself up in the hill of the mountain. Don't stop. DON'T QUIT UNTIL YOU REACH ON THE TOP OF THE MOUNTAIN!

"The only person you are destined to become is the person you decide to be."

—*Ralph Waldon Emerson*

You must change your financial consciousness.

The poor people I met every day used to say, "Why don't you have a family? You're already 30 years old. Look at me, I'm 25 years old and I already have three kids. You're old enough to be a single. Are you a gay?" [They will laugh.]

And I tell 'em, "It's better to be gay than a poor." [I'll laugh inside.]

Poor people always think that the only price they can get is having a child. They often assume that their greatest investment in their life is their children. This is why they are saving money so their children can go to school; to save their lives in the future. I ask them why some of these people are happy with their lives.

"Don't you want to get rich?" I utter.

"I'm too old enough. I have no chance to get rich anymore," they say.

"What do you do with your life right now?" [They cheer some beers.]

"We're happy being together."

Some people fear getting rich so as not to lose their friends. They think if they grew rich, no one knows them anymore. The expression is, "If you become rich, you will lose your friends." It was as if they love their friends so much that they don't want to lose them.

You know what, you became who you wanted to be with. If you do not want to change your financial consciousness, you will get to die with a false belief about money. Some still believe that money can't lead you to heaven. However, if their friends get rich, they still say: He only becomes rich, now he's arrogant. Poor people are always jealous when you get rich, but they never do anything with their lives. They're complicated. Their minds are chaotic. The reason why they have more crimes in poverty is that, people don't care about their lives. All they want is to get in trouble.

Poor people I encounter don't believe in God.

The poor people I've encountered don't believe in

God. Whenever I get dressed and go to church every Sunday, my neighbors say to me: Don't attempt to be so good, for God will take you sooner. I feel like they're looking at me like a stranger. If you ask them, why don't they go to church; so, they can be blessed by God.

They respond, "I don't have time for it."

You know what happens when you don't spend time with God. He will not give you time to prosper. Always remember this: GOD FIRST!

"I will to teach you my ways, and give an undivided heart."
—Psalm 86:11

If you're brilliant, why aren't you wealthy?

Smart people overlooked their weaknesses. They don't even listen to rich people. They still think of rich people as boring. They have several above average IQ, but it's small of numbers that can earn enough. They tend to neglect skills like developing relationships, and focusing on their intelligence. Smart people believe that their success is predetermined by their intelligence, and other abilities are not important. Brilliant children are often told that their intellect is invaluable throughout their childhood. They are told that their intelligence is success comes from easily.

The reason companies hire smart people for knowing their weaknesses. They know that everything known to a smart person is perfectionist. But reality in life, it is better to make mistakes many times so you determine to manage the risks. Being a perfectionist is a lot of thinking before you take risks.

Smart people aren't as patient. They want to be successful early, because they know so much; they've seen so much. They do not think about their weaknesses. They have great expectations of themselves. However, for some industries, raw intelligence isn't enough to succeed. In concentrating beyond your greatest, strength is a result for failures.

Smart people also have difficulty delegating. They believe, they can do something better. Many successful persons lost several times before winning. Learning comes from making mistakes. Successful people know that success is a poor teacher.

> *"Everyone is genius. But if you judge a fish to climb a tree,*
> *it will live it's whole life believing that it is stupid."*
> *—Albert Einstein*

Rich Mindset Activity Action Exercise

1. List down the ten (10) negative belief about money. Make it positive, just like this:

"I am poor," change it to, "I am rich."

"I can't afford it," change it to, "How can I afford it?"

Have a peace of mind about money, and always think that money is very valuable in your life.

2. Make a list of the five (5) right decisions you make in your lifetime. Focus your attention on it. Remember, you have your own choice. If you think it's right, do it. Choose the right decision.

3. Write down the core gift that God has given you a talent in which you are good. Concentrate on it. Make this as a purpose on your daily lives. If you are good at music. Write down what you can do about it to enhance this skill.

4. Bend your arm straight in front of you and make a fist in your hand and say this:

I will become rich!

One more time.

I will become rich!

One more time.

I will become rich!

say it again and again.

Why do poor people have so much debt?

Last night, I was buying a 3n1 coffee at my neighbor's house. They want me to drink some of their beer. I refuse. I said, "No thanks. I have so much work to do which is why I need some coffee to stay awake."

They're inviting me to bet on basketball game. I don't know how to play that game. It was like a card and you choose two numbers to win. It's popular in the Philippines, but I don't really know it.

I reply, "I never play this kind of game, and I don't want to spend my money on it. All the money I've acquired, I've invested in growing into the future."

They said, "You know what, you will become rich one day because you are so kuripot (stingy).

I say, "Yes, I'll be rich!"

The time has come for me to become rich, and I believe in it. They said you had to have a wife to settle in. One way or another, I said, I want to get my wealth before I get married. People may think they were offended by what they hear, even if there is nothing wrong with what I said.

The problem of the poor is that they only want to

hear the mistaken belief. If you're honest and you tell them what's right, you'll be a bad person. I'm still praying to God that I hope I can earn a lot of money, so I won't be here. I don't want to tolerate this kind of people. I don't want to be with that sort of person. My life right now is dangerous. I sense that at any moment, these people will kill me. I feel like they've always hated me; they're so insecure about what I said. It's so hard to live in poverty, because people never understand what you want; all they want is chaos. I can't do what I want. I feel like I'm being controlled by the people around me. I don't have any freedom, since people want to hear what they want. If they hear something positive from you, they will become angry. Their minds are closed to something that can help them out of poverty; they live in a wrong belief. If they hear an opportunity, they criticize immediately. They fear to hear the right thing that could change their lives in the future. Instead, they continue to play gambling that they believe will lift them out of poverty, so they never change. If government said, "Who wants change?" They all raised their hands. But if the government says, "Who wants to change?" No one raised their hands. They want change, but they do not want to help themselves make it.

I want to have a better life. I want to have a rich lifestyle. I want to have everything I want in life. I always pray to God that all my dreams will come true. I will be the happiest person that ever lived. I will be no longer distracted by the people around me. Although I live alone, I have no problem as long as God gives me a wonderful life; as long as he gives me what I want. I deserve a better life. If ever God gives me someone who stay at my side, that's a bonus for me. Which is why I work so hard to make my dream come true and make my dreams happened. Since then, I don't want to be like those guys who just know how to play a gambling.

According to Gambler's Help

Signs of Harm from Gambling

Long before it sounds like a problem, gambling can cause harm.

Harm from gambling isn't just about losing money. Gambling can have an impact on self-esteem, relationships, physical and mental health, work performance and social life. It can harm not only the person who plays, but also family, friends, workplaces and communities. Here are some signs of gambling that you can look for.

Initial Signs of Harm:

❖ Have less time or money to spend for leisure and family.

❖ Reduced savings.

❖ Increased consumption of alcohol.

❖ A sense of guilt or regret.

Advanced Signs of Harm:

❖ Relationship conflict.

❖ Reduced work or study performance.

❖ Financial difficulties.

❖ Anger

Poor people always borrowed money.

I have often experienced it when someone is trying to borrow money from me. Once I refuse, they will be offended. They will insult you if you are not around. Only if you let them borrow, every time they see you, they simply forget your name than those debts. I went through a lot of times when I ran a business. They prefer to borrow instead of paying properly.

It is not a problem for me if people want to borrow money; I am ready to help those in need. Despite that, if you have money on your pocket, you don't use it to pay properly. That is the problem of those who have borrowing habits: ATTITUDE. (Even though you have money or not you still want to pay in debt.)

That's the main reason why my first venture was closed. I had much more listed debt on my notebook, than making a profit. Which is why I always go bankrupt and go back to my old work of selling balut in the street. This is why many businesses are closing as a result of the debt. You know that, when you have so many debts, the world takes everything you have. This includes your time, your work, your home, your life, your trust, even your dignity. If the key element of money, and confident suddenly disappeared, economic collapse like a house of cards. Which is why most of the money nowadays is known as "fiat" money: money that cannot be converted to something tangible like gold or silver.

According to PHYS.ORG

In 2019, consumer debt in the United States reached an all-time high; exceeding for the last time during the 2008 financial crisis. Such debt takes many forms, including mortgages and student loans. But credit card debt alone has surpassed $870 billion, and that's mostly due to discretionary spending. Why are so many Americans needlessly putting themselves in the hole?

The answer could be in the psychological profile of the debtor, says Stéphanie M. Tully. She's an assistant professor of marketing at Stanford Graduate School of Business. In a recent study, Tully and his co-authors found that not all consumers feel the same way about available financing.

"What we found is that people's feelings about the ownership of money can predict their interest in taking on debt," Tully says. "It seems some people are fine with going into debt as long as it doesn't feel like debt."

"There are times when debt can be beneficial," she says. "You invest in a home or higher education. But the choice to go into debt over discretionary purchases isn't a rational calculation, and for many it's suboptimal."

The Psychological Borrowing

Tully and his co-authors, Eesha Sharma from Dartmouth and Cynthia Cryder from Washington University at St. Louis, are the first to explore the "psychological ownership of money" and its link to consumer debt. "Nobody's really tried before to measure this feeling of ownership and its effects on borrowing habits," she says.

The researchers found that the sense of psychological ownership: a concept first used in management literature to describe employee attitudes toward organizations. It is distinct from such factors as debt aversion, financial literacy, income, and self-control, and that it's even more predictive of one's willingness to incur debt. The more consumers feel a sense of ownership overborrowed funds, the more likely they are to use those funds.

"This research suggests that it may be less about understanding the details of compound interest and more about basic attitudes," Tully utters. "If you can change the way people think about borrowed money from an early age, that could make an impact across their lifetime. Credit card companies do a great job of making us feel like they're granting us access to our money. They're not. It's important to understand that this is debt."

Some people treat money as a game. They enjoy gambling money. However, for many people money is not a game; it is survival. Unfortunately, the more civilized we get, the more money becomes a part of our life.

Why poor people struggle financially?

Would you believe that most people are going to be in debt until they die as soon as they leave school?

Have you ever heard these words: Low down payments? Easy monthly payments: Don't worry, the government will give you a tax break for those losses. Then, you know someone is luring you into the game. If you want financial freedom, you must be smarter.

Most people don't have real assets. Things that put money into their pockets, they are often indebted to anyone else. This is why they are clinging to job security and struggle financially.

Get out of debt!

One survey found that seven out of ten Filipino consumers are struggling with debt problems. Making the Philippines the "most stressed" nation when it comes to managing household finances compared with the rest of the Asia-Pacific (APAC); especially during this prolonged COVID-19 pandemic.

Managing debt is a struggle for 70% of consumers in the Philippines. It is their top challenge when it comes to managing their finances.

The share of 70% of Filipino consumers facing debt was highest among the nine surveyed APAC markets; where the average debt-weary consumer ratio was 49%.

Do you know anyone who always goes to 'gimik' (trip); always go to the shopping mall, but had more debts?

Do you know anyone who often posts his 'Out of Towns' on Facebook but has an issue with his finances?

Do you know anyone who are 'Feeling Bless', but the truth is, they are 'Feeling Stress'?

Do you have a friend who only knows you when only if he'll borrow money? But if you don't have money, they don't know you?

The truth is, I never knew in my entire life that I was in debt. If I had borrowed money, I could pay it the day after tomorrow. I never made the habit of being a borrower. If you had that borrowing attitude your financial psychology was so disorderly. You cannot have the peace of having a money, because your mind has too much thinking. You cannot have the peace of people whom you always use to borrow money. Your old friend has now become your enemy.

You ruined the relationship with your friends. If you want to have peace with your money try to keep track of your spending habits. Try budgeting your expenses. Whereas if you knew it was for enjoyment, at the end of the day you have anxiety depression. You can't sleep at night, because you got that mental depression. Did you know that 60% of suicides are committed by people who have mood disorders? There is little energy to plan and implement suicide deep into the depression. About 30% of suicides are committed by individuals with psychiatric disorders other than mood disorders.

Rich Mindset Activity Action Exercise

1. List down the five (5) ways to get out of debts. Start paying all your debts, either to your friends, the company or in credit card. Save at least 30% budget on your monthly income to pay out all your debts.

2. If you're totally debt free, save your money to invest; either in real state, stock market or in your business. I advise you not to invest if you don't repay all your debts.

3. The most important step to becoming debt-free is to stop borrowing money. No more swiping credit cards. No more loans. No more new debts.

4. It's best to track all of your monthly bills for at least a month; as well as daily spending. Don't forget to include your debt payment obligations while tracking.

- ❖ Use a budget worksheet.
- ❖ Keep notes in a notebook.
- ❖ Use a free money management app.
- ❖ Use banking app trackers.
- ❖ Keep receipts

5. Once you've tracked your expenses, it's time for a budget. By using your regular spending as a guide, this budget should account for all of your needs.

6. Bend your arm straight in front of you and make a fist in your hand and say this:

The Mindset of Rich and Poor

I will become rich!
One more time.
I will become rich!
One more time.
I will become rich!
say it again and again.

How the rich generate their income?

School isn't making you rich,
dedication is.

If you were born prior to 1930, then "Go to school, get good grades, and find a safe—secure job," was good advice. But for some, this was the worst advice. Why? In as much as being an employee is like being a 50/50 partner in government. The government takes 50% or more of employees' earnings, and much of that before the employee even sees the pay check.

If you're an employee at the moment and you hate your boss because the promotion you wanted was transferred to someone else; you don't pay him enough. Consequently, you leave your job, 6 months later, you are happy again because you have found a new job. Sadly, the cycle starts again. Your way of life is like a dog chasing his tail.

Sometimes when dogs run after their tails, they simply have fun. They get to know their bodies and find out what they can do. Other times through, tail chasing may be sign of compulsive behavior.

The study shows that compulsive behavior is

behavior that is shown for a longer time than normal. Repeated out of context or repeated in situations are considered abnormal. Compulsive behaviors tend to worsen over time and often require medical or behavioral treatment.

You're trap on money.
Get out of there!

If you have a special someone right now and you fall in love; later you get married. You both are blissful. With a rent to pay, they can afford to set a few moneys to buy a dream of your life. Afterwards you brought a house. Take your money out of your savings, and use it to make a down payment. You have a mortgage, because you do have a new house. You need new furniture, so you go into the store. You now have new furniture to pay monthly.

You put on your friends for parties to see your new house, new car, new furniture and more. Then, the first child was born. Eventually, the child went off to nursery school; the couple must now go to work every day. They are trapped in the need for employment security simply because, on average, they are less than three months away from financial bankruptcy. These two couples often say: I don't have the means to quit. I have bills to pay.

I often say, "I'm going back to school, so I can get a raise." Also, "I am working hard to get a promotion." However, the fact is that their cycle path is mostly boring. They don't have a time freedom.

If you are a father at the moment and you get a promotion by working hard and taking more responsibility. You had less free time for your children. You leave in your house in the morning, and go back home when your children already fall asleep in the evening.

In contrast, if you are a business owner or an investor. If your business or investment is more successful, you have had free time and money. If your business improves, you don't need to work harder. Rather, working more hours to spend on your children.

If your mindset is wrong, you will never attract money

Your money mindset is how you think about money. If you want to focus the positive attitude, we just discussed on money. You must believe that you can master your money; that you can make more money. Invest more money than you make.

Think about wealth and money in a good light. Sometimes rich people are demonized by politics and the media.

In reality, most people who are successful in attracting money today are hardworking—upstanding people. There is nothing wrong with having money, or trying to attract more money than you already have. Don't think that way.

You need to put money on your head all the time.

The reason most people struggle financially is because, they follow the guidance of people who are also mentally blind to money. If you want the money to come to you, you need to know how to care for it. If money isn't the first in your head, it won't stick to your hands.

Savers are Losers

In 1971, President Nixon took the American dollar out of the gold standard; money became debt. The primary reason prices have risen since 1971 is simply because, the United States now has the power to print money to pay its bills.

Since 1971, the United States dollar has lost 95% of its value against gold. It will take no more than 40 years to lose the remaining 5%. During this year, gold is $35 an ounce. Forty years later, it was worth $1,400 an ounce. This is the mass loss of the purchasing power of the dollar.

As a Federal Reserve Bank and Central Bank throughout the world, print trillions of dollars at high speed. Every printed dollar means higher taxes and more inflation.

The Philippine Peso History

The 1946 U.S Bell Trade Act was established there at the end of the American rule. In the years that followed, our imports (which led to dollar outflow) exceeded our exports (source of dollar inflows). The gap widened over time.

President Diosdado Macapagal eventually let the peso seek its natural level in the 1960s. Which led the peso to lose nearly half its value, at P3.90 to the dollar.

Let us look at the 1990s, when the government eased controls on the foreign exchange market. The exchange rate was about P26 to P27 to the dollar. When the Asian crisis hit, the exchange rate went beyond the P40 almost overnight. The BSP subsequently declared that its main policy was the control of inflation, rather than influencing the exchange rate.

In 2005, the exchange rate attained its highest level ever, namely P56. When the financial crisis struck Western economies in 2008, investment funds took refuge in the 'emerging markets' of the East. Boosting foreign exchange supplies faster than we could spend it.

In the past two years, though, the peso has been an odd man out. From P42 to the dollar in 2013, the rate changed successively to P44, P45, P47, P50 and now P53. Our neighbors' currencies have generally appreciated, reflecting their healthy export growth of up to 25% per annum.

Rich Mindset Activity Action Exercise

1. Focus on all three (3) net worth factors: increasing your income, increasing your return on investment, and decreasing your cost of living by simplifying your lifestyle.

2. List your three (3) biggest worries, concerns or fears regarding money and wealth. Challenge them. For each, write down what you should do if the situation you fear really occurs. Could you still survive? Could you make a comeback? Chances are the answer is yes. Now quit worrying and start getting rich.

3. Get educated. Take investment seminars. Read at least one investment book a month. Read magazines such as Money, Forbes, Barron's and Wall Street Journal. Then, choose an arena to become an expert in. Begin your investment in this arena.

4. Bend your arm straight in front of you and make a fist in your hand and say this:

I will become rich!

One more time.

I will become rich!

One more time.

I will become rich!

say it again and again.

Rich people are successful, Poor people are unsuccessful

The Road Not Taken
By: Robert Frost

Two roads diverged in a yellow wood,
And sorry I could not travel both
And be one traveler, long I stood
And looked down one as far as I could
To where it bent in the undergrowth;

Then took the other, as just as fair,
And having perhaps the better claim,
Because it was grassy and wanted wear;
Though as for that the passing there
Had worn them really about the same,

And both that morning equally lay

In leaves no step had trodden black.

Oh, I kept the first for another day! Yet knowing how way leads on to way, I doubted if I should ever come back.

I shall be telling this with a sigh

Somewhere ages and ages hence:

Two roads diverged in a wood, and I— I took the one less traveled by,

And that has made all the difference.

Why poor people are unsuccessful?

Poor people are always saying that, "I took pity on you." They took pity on others, but they didn't realize they sympathize more than they think. They didn't realize that their life is such a struggle. If you are truly ashamed of the person, you do not have to say it. Instead, you help them. You got so much to say to someone, but you never help him. Be careful with your words, because it is painful as a sharp sword.

I had an experience when I was working as a service crew, the manager who hired me said, "Kung hindi lang ako naaawa sa'yo, Jo. Hindi talaga kita ipapasok dito." (If only I don't pity you. I'll never hire you here.). Somehow in my mind, why accept me in my job initially, if that's all I've heard. When she told me that, it was at that point that I was no longer interested in my work. My ego got beat up and I thought that I worked here for nothing but shame. It hurt my ego. I feel like I've been working so hard with my tears, my blood, my sweat out of pity.

Those are the start that I lose my interest for my job. One week later, I resigned because of this. For about a year of work as a service crew, I move four jobs in different establishment. In every work I took, I encountered a problem with my co-workers. That's when I realized I wasn't born to work. The number one problem of my job is not my job; these are my co-workers. As an employee, I have experienced so many situations that my co-workers do not treat me well. Especially when you're in a low-level position. You are so oppressed by ahead of you.

People are so arrogant if you're in the low-level position. Thus, if you promote in the higher position, they come up with ways to bring you back to your previous position. Poor people are always jealous if someone gets promoted. Still, if they are promoted, they are happy that others remain in their low-level position. It was like they didn't want to be outdone. They always tell the world they've won. They tell everybody they're being promoted. They're self-centered. They just want them to do whatever it takes not to lose.

They didn't realize that people around them aren't appreciated. They feel like the world loves them so much, even if nobody loves them because of their actions. They may want to impress others. They feel that they are happy with what they are doing, but at the end of the day, they are not. If you get a promotion about your work, you don't need to tell everyone that you are increasing your level. Be grateful and thankful that God has placed you there, because you have been blessed more than the people around you. You don't need to impress everyone that you have changed. If that position comes back to you and you go back to your old level, you're force to quit on your job. Given that the people around you that you work with, they see you as something different. You do whatever it takes going up to win in the corporate ladder. But at the end of the day, your boss is going to get richer on your hard work.

"You need to be a creator rather than a competitor. You will get what you want, but in such a way that when you do, every other man will have more than he has now."

—Wallace D. Wattles

Be kind to each other, even if you are in a low-level position or in a higher position. You're not here to go up against each other. You're there to work as a team. If your only motivation is to compete with your fellow employees, you seem to win. But deep down, you're the loser. You enjoy your work, don't be so stressed out.

Blaming other people won't make you successful in life.

My brother chatted me on Facebook last night. He said that he never wanted to see our mother again. Due to her his life is untidy. As he told me, "Do you remember Jo she neglecting us, as we are a child whom she put herself first? She is selfish. I don't want to see her anymore. I never saw her as a true mother. I hate her. Because of her, my life is ruined because she hasn't looked after us well since our childhood. All she wants is for herself.

But he never realized how much she had done to give us a better life. She became a prostitute to feed her children, and it hurt so much when I see his message. For he blamed our mother for his misfortune. You have no right to blame anyone else for your mistakes. As first and foremost, you are the only one who owes your life. You're the only one in control of it. I have failed so many times in my life; even in my education. Thus, I never blamed my mother for all she could. She did whatever she could to give everything we wanted as a mother; even if she's the only one who takes care of us.

I remember my mom when I was in high school. I was failing in my subject matter, and she went to our school. She begs my teacher to pass my exam. Still, I was failing. They don't allow me to pass, even my mother beg so much. When I saw my mother begging for my grades, deep down, I felt so much pain. That time, I realized that you can never please anyone in this world. Unfortunately, if you want to get help from someone, nothing will help you. But if you don't care about people around you, everyone loves you.

People who live in this world are better at hurting a lot of times than begging someone not to get hurt. My mother was a good person. She did everything she could for her children, even if she died for us. Nothing beats love of a mother. For me, the only superhero in this world is my mother. The love of Mother cannot be replaced even how much the value it is.

My brother is an unsuccessful person who just wants to give his children a good life, and don't care about the other things in life. If he wants to give a better life to his children, he needs to grow as an individual. Blaming someone won't make you succeed in life. You do a lot of things in your family, but you do nothing to make yourself better.

If you want to grow, you need to get rid of the past. If you stay on the person from your past, you're the same person that you were. Not everything in this world is right. Humans are born out of mistakes in life; it's natural for us to make mistakes.

"Being filled with unrighteousness, wickedness, greed, evil, full of envy, murder, strife, deceit, and malice. They are gossip, slanders, haters of God, insolent, arrogant, boastful."

— Romans 1:29

All you need is to learn to forgive and forget. You must surrender your heart to have peace in life. We are not perfect human beings; we're all born sinful. You just have to learn to love others, no matter how painful it may be. If you live in this world with hatred, all the people that surround you will never make you a real person. If you want to be more mature, just focus on what's good for you and your loved ones. If you want to change the life of your loved ones in the future, you need to change first.

My brother says, "You're on your own in this world. You have no family. You have no friends. You have no one to comfort you. For you will be die alone forever. I replied, "It's okay. At least my heart is at peace."

If you want to get rich, change your attitude

My brother will never get rich if they just know to hate the people around him. He'll stick on his negative mindset forever, if he doesn't grow up. As an investor I need to have friends. A group that can seek advice from my mentors about which stocks to buy; which stocks to sell. With the advice of others, I can lessen my failure. They were the only ones who ever thought about me and guided me. For me, two heads are better than one. You should ask someone who did. If you think that you know everything in life, you don't seek someone's help. Your learnings are limited. If you think you're smart, you can't take advantage of your passion. If you are the only one doing it, you should surround it in the same passion as you do.

My brother knows everything. When I encourage him to invest in stock markets, he said, "I already know what the stock market is, you don't have to ask me out on that. I lost two million pesos in the stock market last month. Don't believe that. Never think on the investors that they told you, because they are the same. All they want with you is to get you scammed."

He didn't realize that, because of what he was saying, this is the same person he is right now. He did not grow, for he believes only in his confidence. It is better to know other people's mistakes, so you can determine the risk.

When Amazon founder Jeff Bezos asked Warren Buffet: You are the second richest man in the world. Your investment thesis is simple. Why doesn't anyone copy you?

He replied, "Because nobody wants to get rich slow."

That's what teamwork is, they get rich slowly but surely. The key to long-term stock market investment is to buy "on sell" and have the patience to wait.

Prevention is better than cure. Don't let yourself experience what they did to everyone else. You must invest in yourself before you can make your decision. You have to study first; take courses to know how to fight risk. You weren't born into the world where you already know everything. You need someone to coach you; someone to guide you. Just as to learn how to ride a bicycle, the first try is that you will fall. The second time you'll crash. The third time you lose. That's how you can learn. However, if you had someone to guide you, you can prevent or less it all.

If you do not suppress your hatred for anyone, you will eliminate the goodness and kindness around you. You will never learn to appreciate their wisdom. As your heart is filled with scarcity. Your mind will not be able to open a new opportunity. Remember, learning comes from listening, feelings and action. It begins with the heart, mind, and soul. If you can forget about using it, your mind will be closed forever.

"Weakness of attitude, becomes weakness of character."

—Albert Einstein

The life without limbs.

I remember the man who had no arms, and no legs. Nick James Vujicic is an Australian American Christian evangelist and motivational speaker born with tetra-amelia syndrome: a rare disorder characterized by the absence of arms and legs.

His doctor told that his not gonna walk. He's not going to go to school. He's not gonna do anything for himself. His parents told him, "You're going to try this, try this, and that." They give him a lot of encouragement and love. For he goes to school. Everyone swears it, and compares it to the way he looks. They always teased him when he was in school. Saying, "You can't do this, and you can't do that. You have nothing to do with your life."

Vujicic is a 21-year-old graduate of Griffith University with a Bachelor of Commerce degree; having a double major in Accounting and Financial Planning.

A disability is not a barrier to succeed in life. Many people do not have disabilities, but they face too many obstacles in their lives.

"The problem is not the problem.

The problem is your attitude towards the problem."

—Captain Jack's Sparrow

I saw so many poor people on the street with full physique, but they were only lying on the floor. They're waiting for someone to hand them something. Poor people only know how to rely on other people. They're not trying to survive. They just want to wait for somebody to help them. When no one helps them, they say,

"Help us because we are poor, we are getting poorer because of the rich people." It's like we're running out of money in the world that we can't print money again.

The weight you carry cannot be measured. It is measured by the quantity of what you can do. What you're carrying is going to be even heavier, if you can't find a way to make it easier. If you feel you can't, just think of other people with disabilities.

People have so much excuse when it comes to taking action. They do not even realize that all things might happen, if they simply do something. Any poor person knows there's a reason.

Researchers at the University of Florida have discovered that making too many excuses will likely lead others to doubt your sincerity, sabotage your personal goals and make you more self-absorbed.

You can't do nothing in this world if you're just sitting on the ground. If you do not find a way to get up, you are sitting on that ground forever. Just as the man at Sabbah. Jesus Christ healed the man at that place. He wasn't able to walk for 38 years, but when Jesus spoke he was healed at once. He doesn't take the man to get up. He told the man, "Take up your bed, and walk." He didn't help the man to get up, instead he told him to get up. He never said, "You seem so miserable. I'll help you stand. Come, and I'll lift you up. Put your hands on my shoulder.) Instead, he said, "Take your bed and walk."

You are the only person who can help you in getting things to happen. If you don't know how to lift yourself up, you'll never know how to make things happen. If your reason is your situation not to take action, that moment will remain that way forever.

"Success is not something happens to you, it something happens because of you and because of the action you take"

—Grant Cardone

The rich never believe in luck.

Rich people never think things will happen. They know is, they have to do so much work and effort. No wonder millionaires wake up early, while most poor people still sleep and begin to plan their day. The rich won't waste their time at the casino. They don't expect a miracle to happen, even though this is hard work. Making them the right decision still pays off. That is how the rich gain success and wealth by coming up with ideas. Investing on it and working hard to succeed. This process may not be seamless, but with patience, self-discipline and perseverance, they made it.

"What's the point, if someone says he has faith but has no works? Can that faith save him?"

—James 2:14

Rich Mindset Activity Action Exercise

1. Make a list of ten (10) people whom it would be helpful for you to know. Write each of them congratulation on something they have just done

2. List five (5) or more people you hate, and who have done something wrong with your life. Contact or meet them in person. Apologies to them and say sorry about your misunderstanding. Be humble, because at the end of the day, you still have nothing to do if you don't apologize. It's better to live peacefully, and focus on your goals.

3. Make a list of ten (10) names that you want to forgive; those who did something to your life in the past. It's either your old co-workers or friends. If you want to succeed in life, do not cultivate anger to someone. After that, place it to your mail box.

4. Write in your daily journal that you are grateful and thankful to God that you are achieving something. Make it as your daily goals.

5. Make a to do list. Plan your first day in the morning. Remember, 1-minute saves 10 minutes of executions.

6. Pick one goal that you want to accomplish within 24 hours.

7. Work at those goals all the time.

8. Resist the temptation to clear up small things

9. Bend your arm straight in front of you and make a fist in your hand and say this:

I will become rich!
One more time.
I will become rich!
One more time.
I will become rich!
say it again and again.

Why poor people are staying poor and broke?

"The world is a dangerous place. Not because of those who do evil, but because of those who look on and do nothing"

— Albert Einstein

Why poor people are hard to deal with?

You can't please a poor person's poverty. Most of them are selfish and afraid about losing something. They are afraid of helping someone. For them, helping someone is too much to lose for them. Which is why all the poor people knows is to say the bad words so they don't lose something. This is why they are still poor. The only ability they have is to ignore other people and hate them.

The big reason for the poor is that they don't get along when you need to. All they come up with is how to get a problem. They don't think of the solution. They do everything they want to do to create a problem. Even if you're not doing something, they come to you and look for problems. They don't do anything with their lives, all they know is an issue. They find means of affecting you. The problem with poor people is being arogant and makes problems. They find ways of insulting you. It seems that they were looking for attention on you. Some of them are members of fraternity; they are not afraid of something. Every time they get into trouble, they can always get help with their brotherhood.

How come the poor are irresponsible?

Last afternoon, I went to the toilet; it's dirty. There's a poop inside the bowl. I can't clean it up, because it's not my responsibility. In the poverty zone, they always said, "I use the restroom, you clean my waste." Instead of taking a bath, I decided not to. The reason the poor are a lot poorer is that they're irresponsible. They want others to care for their mess or dirt. That's why poor people will never grow. They're never going to get rich, since they don't even care about small things. If one is irresponsible about small things, one is irresponsible about big things. If you really want to grow, don't allow others to clean up your mess.

All poor people want is to get rich. However, becoming rich starts by taking on more responsibility. You start with your own self. You start with a good attitude. Because whenever you get rich, but if your attitude remains poor, others don't think you're not. For this reason, lottery winners will become rich. Still, their attitude is not. They start out with more money, than gaining with more responsibility.

You should take responsibility for everything around you, even if you are rich or poor. People will treat you well. They will respect you for your attitude. This is not about how to get rich, the question is, who you will become by getting rich?

Why drunk people are very hard to deal with?

Last night, I was dealing with a drunk people. All the drunk knows is that they don't want to lose. Even if you explain yourself thoroughly. All they want is to shut your mouth. It doesn't only happen to a drunk, it happens to a poor person. They don't want you to explain anything. To them, they are always right. In their eyes, if you explain it to them, you'll lose their respect. They want other people to respect them, but they have no respect for themselves. Sometimes, it's so hard if you're a silent type person. Everyone thinks that you're a coward. Thus, sometimes silence comes as a judgement. There is nothing wrong with judgment, because you only use your mind to see the attitude of a person. The advantages of being an introvert is the ability to study a person's weakness.

All a drunk man knows is to be an arrogant, sometimes it's irritating because they keep talking. If they're too drunk, they speak a foreign tongue. Therefore, I am not with them anymore. The lesson I've learned is that people like that should not be tolerated. It ruined your life. I can say that I've wasted so much time with these kinds of people. If this time I use it to be with a nourishing people, perhaps I shall become successful today.

If I'm already surrounded by a mindful person, I don't have a lot of regrets at the moment. But that happens, you must learn from the past before you realize your mistakes. Still, this time, I will leave no one in control of my life. It's time to change. It's time to learn more. This is the moment to surround myself with good people. If you do something, you make mistakes, and our mistakes teach us the most. Remember that anything important can't really be learned in school. It must be learnt by taking action, making mistakes, and then correct them. That's how wisdom sets in.

I advise you, if these people will always be with you every day, you are close for a psychological barrier. In the study of the University of Chicago, the ability of these people is limited. The memory curve is a decay, and the attention focuses only on one at a time.

If you have always been with these people you are near crimes. They suffer from poor retention, distrust, neglect, and anger. You put yourself into danger. It's better to stay away for these people unless you want to ruin your life. Be with the people who always strive for excellence, not with the people who always strive for crimes.

Did you know that?

As of March 2019, the majority of inmates in the National Bilibid Prison in the Philippines were local. The Philippines ranks 5th among Asia's largest incarcerated population. A total of approximately 200,000 inmates as of August 2020.

It's so hard if you're from this population because inside the prison you can't do what you want. You can't fulfil your dreams anymore. Do you want it to happen with you?

If God give you time to focus on your goals; make the most out of it. Do not waste your time for things you might not benefit from. You will never become happy with your bad habits. Instead, focus your attention on the advancement of your dreams. At the end of the day, your bad habits friends will not be with you in difficult moments. They're there when spending. When you went any amount out of your pocket, they will also be gone.

How to please poor people?

You cannot please the poor people. I've experienced a lot of time whenever my neighbors are so noisy. Every time, I read books, I cannot concentrate. My mind was so distracted; all I can do is to please them. Hoping that they can minimize their voice. Thus, they just replied, "Why are you stopping us?" In a poverty zone, you can't stop people from getting noisy. It's too much noise here. If you want peace, go live on the subdivision.

In my head, if I have a lot of money right now, I don't live here anymore. I will transfer right away. If my investments are growing and making a profit, I will no longer be here. There is no way to please a person who cannot understand what peace is. I said to myself, "Just bear with it, Jo. The time has come when you go away in here." Time will come. I can live somewhere peaceful and beautiful place.

There will come a time when I can concentrate my

reading without any distraction. It's so hard to be with a people with no consideration. You can't please or you don't have a right to control them. Considering you don't own the place. It is better to have one's own place, so that people around you will be considered.

Being distracted by a noise is very annoying. Not only that, you miss the important lessons. As well, your interest in what you read is going to go away. All I can say is that it's better to live in the underground with nobody to be with. So that you can focus on your work, because I'm kind of an easily distracted person. I don't want other people making noise. Therefore, I may finish my work immediately and less time; move on to another task. Twenty-four hours a day, it's not enough for me to finish all my work. If you are a productive person, you want your work to accomplish immediately. Since you can have more time on the other things.

Rich Mindset Activity Action Exercise

1. Meet a friend or family who can support you. Tell that person that you want to speak about the power of commitment in order to create greater success. Put your hands on your heart. Look at this person in the eye; repeat the following:

I, (your name), do hereby commit to become rich by (date). Thank you!

2. Write about the problem you have in your life. Then hear about the specific steps you can take to resolve, or at least improve this situation. This will give you an insight into the problems. First, there's a big chance that you'll solve the problem. Second, you will feel a lot better.

3. Practice getting out of your comfort zone. Intentionally make decisions that are uncomfortable for you. Speak to someone you wouldn't normally talk to. Request a raise for job or high prices in your business. Wake up an hour earlier each day. Walk in the woods at night. Take an enlightened warrior training. It will train you to be unstoppable!

4. Bend your arm straight in front of you and make a fist in your hand and say this:

I will become rich!

One more time.

I will become rich!

One more time.

I will become rich!
say it again and again.

Rich people are eco-friendly, poor people are eco-enemies

"History is written by the rich, and so the poor are blamed for everything."

— Jeffrey D. Sachs

Poor people love throwing garbage on the street.

The primary reason for a flood is garbage in the street. Whenever people throw garbage, it goes into the hole that causes blockage and in each lake the water cannot flow into the river. If people are concerned about how to separate their waste, we have no problem with our environment. If people care about the appropriate way to throw away their trash, our ecological system will become much healthier. The more we clean our environment, the clearer our river; seems like the ocean. Also, the cleaner our environment, the more we can breathe fresh air. Knowing that our trees can grow much more. In fact, according to the study conducted by Ocean Conservancy, the main reason of plastic leakage into the ocean is waste that is still not collected.

Earlier this year, a World Bank report found that globally about 4.8 to 12.7 million tonnes of mismanaged plastic enters the ocean each year. Of that amount, about 80% comes from Asia. However, the Philippines alone contributes an estimated 0.75 million tonnes of plastic waste in the ocean; third-largest contributor globally.

According to figures from the Department of Environment and Natural Resources, only 30% of baranggay in the country segregate waste.

I've always seen a lot of poor people on the street who are in the habit of throwing garbage. When they finish their meal, they enjoy dumping their waste wherever they go. They do not realize that a bottle of mineral water can recycle billions of plastic wastes to produce packaging materials. If people care about recycling, a lot of people can help our world become much healthier; saving lives for many animals across the globe. I encounter numerous times when I was selling balut (duck egg), the eggshells are just throwing anywhere. I provide them with a plastic that's to be used when throwing eggshells, but they didn't follow me. They never listened to me. They were prepared to throw it into the street. They say, "It's okay. No one will get mad at you. I can handle this. People here are afraid of me." Many of my customers are influenced by alcohol. When they end up hanging out, they like to eat balut. But most balut vendors, the biggest problem they face every day is sober people. They risk their lives in the streets and are still vulnerable to bullying.

The UK government has announced its goal of recycling 65% of municipal waste by 2035. England, Northern Ireland and Scotland failed to meet their EU target of 50% recycling rate in 2020. This aggressive change by the government is necessary for us to achieve this attainable goal.

Protecting ecosystems and wildlife.

Recycling reduces the need to cultivate, harvest or remove new raw materials from the Earth. This in turn reduces disruption and harm to the natural world: fewer forests cut down, rivers diverted, wild animals harmed or displaced, and less pollution of water, land and air.

In addition, of course, if our plastic waste is not secured in recycling, it can be blown or washed into rivers and the sea. They end up hundreds or thousands of miles away, pollute our coasts and waterways and become a problem for everybody.

According to the Public and Environmental Health Effects of Plastic Wastes Disposal

Between 1950 and 2018, some 6.3 billion tonnes of plastic were produced worldwide. About 9% and 12% of this waste was recycled and incinerated, respectively. The increase in the human population and the constant demand for plastics and plastic products are responsible for the continued increase in plastic production. This production of plastic waste and the resulting environmental pollution.

Why is recycling important to a business?

One of the key reasons recycling is important for a business is that, it's a simple way to save money and improve your bottom line. Recycling programs can reduce costs and, best of all, free up money for other sustainable initiatives. Recycling can save major money for your business and save the planet at the same time. It's a win win!

As recycling technology advances, our metals, plastics and glass become increasingly valuable as the cost of materials grows. Recyclable materials are a commodity, so learn about the market value in your region; discover how much your recyclables are worth.

New unpublished research by Lightspeed, commissioned by Rubbermaid Commercial Products, found that sustainability and workplace recycling are more important for millennials than previous generations.

Recycling saves energy.

Of course, another reason that recycling is important for a business is because of the positive environmental impacts. Reusing and recycling materials requires less energy than producing the same materials from scratch. For example, newspaper is recycled to be reused for printing. As when aluminium cans and bottles are recycled, we can save 95% of the energy used to produce those cans relative to the raw materials.

The EPA fact sheet indicates that our landfills are filled with the following wastes that could be easily recycled:

21% of food, the largest component of landfill

14% of paper and card board

10% of rubber, leather, and textiles

18% of plastic

Prevent Global warming

Did you know that pulp and paper is the 5th largest industrial energy consumer in the world? Instead, paper recycling consumes 65% less energy than generating new paper products from raw materials. Once we reduce energy consumption, we reduce our greenhouse gas emissions.

When we recycle 1 ton of paper, we save 17 trees who are playing a vital role in protecting our planet.

Saving and making money from recycling

CEBU, Philippines - In recent years there has been an aggressive campaign to reduce human consumption of things. The crusade stems from the fact that global resources are rapidly depleting as a result of the rapidly growing human population and waste. The term 'Reduce, Reuse, Recycle' has become a global motto.

From time to time, they get it from their friends and relatives. Thus, there may be no need to buy plastic bottles for making crafts.

Nine (9) Ways to Start Crafting

Recycled Materials

1. Plastic Bottle Bracelets

➢ This cute bracelet is perfect for any teenager and is made by re-using bottles of soda or water.

2. Terrarium

➢ Two-litre bottles can be reused or repurposed by turning them into a terrarium. It's a perfect craft for kids.

3. Aqua Spikes

➢ Drip watering helps avoid runoff and allows water to be absorbed deep into the soil to reach the roots of the plant. Reusing plastic bottles to accomplish a win-win situation.

4. Coin Purse

➢ The clever reusing of plastic bottles to create a purse is quite ingenious. It is reminiscent of a little monster that could be adorned with eyes and a nose.

5. Knitting Loom

➢ Larger plastic bottles can be re-used to make these awesome knitting looms. How many people would have thought of doing a knitting craft using recycled plastic?

6. Artsy Box

➢ It is another crafty and cool way to weave plastic to make art. Green plastic is used and woven together to form a box.

7. Privacy Screen

➢ On first glance, it is hard to believe that it is plastic. It looks like glass. This is a beautiful reusing plastic bottles in the house to make a privacy screen.

8. Crafty Vase

➢ This is a cute, crafty and inspiring way to turn a

piece of trash into art. Nobody would ever know these cute beads were ever an old bottle (unless you tell them). Bracelets, necklaces, or bead curtains would all look wonderful crafted from these spectacular plastic bottle beads.

9. Ottoman Chair

➢ With a little bit of creativity and patience, useful stuffs can be made with something that is going to be discarded. This ottoman is not fancy at all, but it's something that can be made with recycled plastic bottles.

Rich Mindset Activity Action Exercise

1. Start saving and collecting recycled materials. You should not buy a plastic bottle for crafts; just get it to your friends and family. Then, start your creativity. If you have skills to create something, this is the advantage for you. Start making money out of your crafts.

2. Write it down, "I'll never throw any more trash in the street. If I can't find any trash cans around me, I keep them until I see one." Only dogs are litter on the street. Are you a dog?

3. Make your surroundings clean green, even your room, your house or office. Remember, cleanliness starts with you. If you want to succeed in life, be responsible.

4. Buy three trash cans at home and start segregating garbage. Put the name into each trash can at: biodegradable, non-biodegradable, and hazardous.

5. Bend your arm straight in front of you and make a fist in your hand and say this:

I will become rich!

One more time.

I will become rich!

One more time.

I will become rich!

say it again and again.

Poor people have scarcity mindset. Rich people have rich mindset

Poor people think miserable.

People expect you to be wrong, but they never believe you're doing right as well. They still think they're correct all the time. I got a neighbor next to my room; we shared the toilet because we're on the same roof. I noticed he was waiting for me to say something harsh. Each time I go to the bathroom to take a bath, there's always a poop in the bowl. He's the only person that uses the toilet. It was like he intentionally never flushed the toilet. He's waiting for my reaction, because he knows I was next person who will go to the bathroom. I've noticed that this person just wants me to be the only one who wants to clean up his waste. Even the next day, the poop was still there; he never took it out. It was like there was something seriously wrong with that person. Considering that every day I saw poop inside the bowl.

The problem with poor people is that they're waiting for something bad to happen. All they want is to make chaos. This is why the poverty field is a very miserable place. Knowing that those who live there have terrible problems. All they know is how to find a problem.

If you always think of yourself as a bad boy; you're right about that. Which is why you're still what you are right now, because all you know is being evil and bad. Poor people still think that being bad is cool. No, you're not cool. You shouldn't be respected in this community. You deserve to rotten in jail. You are just a plague to society.

Why have poor people always complained? about the price?

Poor people always complain about price variations. The only thing they can say is, "It costs a lot now. Yesterday, I purchased the product at a cheaper price; it was charged more." Poor people are very hard to deal with. Since, they are going to get angry if they know that the price increase. It was as if they wanted things to be free. That is the problem with someone who didn't know about the inflation. They have no idea what inflation is, because they were unaware of the changes in the economics of their surroundings. All they know is that the prices for the goods they bought 10 years ago are the same as they are today. They did not see the economic changes.

Do you know our money keeps dropping every year? When the time of Cory Aquino, the price of 1 kg of 'galunggong' is only 25 pesos. But did you know how much one kilo of 'galunggong' costs these days? It's 250 pesos! It's more expensive than 'dalagang bukid' and 'tilapya'.

I just gave you a perpective. Galunggong is a meal

of the 'maralita' or otherwise known as, an ordinary man. It's an affordable meal for poor people. But now it's the food of the rich people.

With inflation rising, our money is decreasing. The inflation rate per year is increasing to 5% per year. So, over the next 10 years, the money is going to drop by 40% to 50%. Plus, the fact, inflation increases, so it will expand our money in two directions: One is going up and the second is going down. It's like a spaghetti that you can stretch upward and downward.

You must widen your memory.

Poor people have no idea that their money is not worth as much as it was years or months ago. They have not grown up, because their minds were stuck in the past. They don't have time to study the changes of the market. You know what, if you don't care about the changes in your surroundings, you'll be left behind. The time has come for you to have no idea that all the people around you are becoming rich. You do not understand why you are still poor, because you do not know how to observe the changes in your surroundings. We should be aware of what will happen around us, knowing that we do not know when the opportunity has arisen. The worst part is, you could just wake up and no one lives in this world. You seem to be the only one living here, because you can't interact with other people. Look around you. Observe what are the changes.

Remember, Kepler Space is looking for the planet at this time; at the possibility of homes for humans. Our future lies in outer space; 100 years from now. It's possible that there is no human being in this world. You got no idea what's about to happen. You need to widen your perspective, because we are more in development today than we have been in recent decades and centuries. The human brain is more focused right now on technology. You must upgrade your memory, since our world is more enhancing right now. You should develop your mind, for you will not left behind.

Poor people always listen to bad news.

Why are we so interested in bad news, anyway? University of Queensland psychologist, Roy F. Baumeister, and his colleagues have noted that, "bad is stronger than good." Humans have a 'negativity bias', in which we pay more attention to negative than positive information.

Unfortunately, the impact of current events on our wellbeing is also particularly important during periods of crisis. Multiple studies have found that, the more we consume news during or after a tragedy, crisis or natural disaster, the more likely we are to develop symptoms of Post-traumatic Stress Disorder (PTSD).

The repeated presentation of information can create cognitive distortions. Meaning, we are likely to interpret worthy problems, such as violent crime; as more prevalent than they really are.

Research published this year has shown that, when we perceive daily news as negative, we may feel less positive as a whole. It is no wonder that increased consumption of news may affect our well-being.

Those who use social media largely for news, instead of social networks, show increased anxiety and depression. These findings emphasize the importance of being strategic in the use of social media, particularly in times of crisis.

Take control of your news consumption.

Our biases mean we're more likely to be impacted by negative news. We tend to believe that what we see is more prevalent than it truly is.

It certainly does not mean that any news is not good news. The news is powerful and keeps you connected and informed. In a way, in a world where we are surrounded by news 24/7, it is important that we are aware of our cognitive biases and the distortions they create. Let's take control of our news consumption, rather than allowing it to control us.

Rich Mindset Activity Action Exercise

1. Take note of "Seven days without complaining." Place it in your mirror, your board, or in your wall. You must do this within 7 days, the next 7 days, and the following 7 days. Until it becomes a habit.

2. Think of yourself as a role model for others; showing yourself to be kind, generous, loving and rich.

3. Control your news consumption. It's better not to care about the news; just focus only on your goals.

4. Bend your arm straight in front of you and make a fist in your hand and say this:

I will become rich!

One more time.

I will become rich!

One more time.

I will become rich!

say it again and again

Why you must get rich?

"The good life is expensive. There is another way to live that doesn't cost as much, but it isn't 'any good."

—Spanish Distiller's

If you're just a poor no one cares about you

When I used to sell in the street, people don't care about you. It was as if you were invisible. They will ignore you, and talk to another person while you are still speaking. It was as if they had no one around them. It's so hard if you're just poor, because people are so arrogant and most of them are under the influenced of alcohol. They feel like they are so rich. They don't want to talk to the poor. But the truth is that they are poorer than any poor people. Since, the real rich do not choose in the person to whom they talk to. However, the poor are so arrogant and act as if they were.

We need to respect each other even if you're rich or not. Besides, you don't have anything to lose if you respond. This is the problem of the poor, they fear to lose something. That is why they preferred not to take the response, because they want to put themselves first. That's the main problem of their attitude. If you don't care about others, they don't care about you either. If you always put yourself on top, you're remaining not to appreciate others. Especially when you are in a business field, if you do not care about others around you, you will never make any profit. Why? It's because you look down the people around you. You give no value to your customer or other people. This is the best asset you should have. Even if you have plenty of information about your business, if your attitude isn't good, all the knowledge that you have is worthless. You need to response respectfully. For we humans are created to make socialize. You'll never know someone else unless you respect them. As listening is more powerful than a sharper memory. If you only want to talk to a few, your learnings are limited, because you always consider yourself higher than other people. Remember, if you are the smartest on the group, you're in the wrong group.

Why hospitals don't care about you when you're poor?

Have you already experienced these on your life that you will fall ill and rush to the hospital? When you get there, no nurse or doctor will notice you. You're waiting for an hour to call your name. When they call you, they talk to you in five minutes and just leave you with a prescription.

According to the Brooking Report

The COVID-19 pandemic has sparked a wave of

public appreciation for the country's frontline heroes. From television ads, firefighter salutes to essential toys for workers. Although doctors and nurses deserve our praise, they are not alone in risking their lives during this pandemic. In fact, they represent less than 20% of all essential health workers.

Unlike the higher-paid doctors and nurses, they work alongside. These essential workers are risking their lives during the pandemic—but with far less prestige and recognition; very low pay, and less access to the protective equipment that could save their lives.

They spoke with pride about their work, but few felt respected. Even when they put their lives at risk, many expressed frustrations, and in some cases—anger; over their lack of life-saving protective equipment.

If you are like many people, you can wait over an hour as if nothing had happened. It was like, "Okay lang. Marami kasing pasyente kaya busy sila." (It's okay. There are many patients, reason why they're busy.) Even though your life was near to death, still it was acceptable for you.

National Nurses United (NNU) has launched a campaign to protest the patient safety risks inherent in EHR use and the detrimental impact of accountable care reforms on how patients receive inpatient care. Representing a number of state and local nursing organizations, NNU decries the "unchecked proliferation" of EHR technology and the "severe risk of harm" brought about by attempts to significantly reduce hospital admissions; shift care to primary care providers and outpatient settings.

You must become rich in order to provide your family a medical assurance. So, by the time the emergency arrives, you can insure your family for medical treatment. Don't expect a government health insurance. They only give you the least benefit that you expected. Don't let your family be a part of this. Do not rely on the benefits of the government; rely on yourself for your family's life.

You need money to live in outer space.

"Saving our planet, lifting people out of poverty, advancing economic growth... these are one and the same fight."

— Ban Ki-moon,

8th Secretary-General of the United Nations

Ticket for Space

❖ Virgin Galactic

➢ $250,000 per ticket on the edge of space includes a space suit.

❖ Passenger

➢ $55 million SpaceX's mission on the Issue; get sleeping bags, and hygiene products.

❖ Blue Origin

➢ $28 million spaceflights come with a seat next to Jeff Bezos.

Richard Branson is scheduled to launch into Virgin Galactic VSS Unity on Sunday for the company's first fully equipped rocket test flight.

If the launch goes according to plan, it will be 9 days ahead of Amazon founder Jeff Bezos. The one that plans to travel to the edge of space on July 20 Blue Origin New Shepard spacecraft.

You must become rich, as everyone right now are focusing on the red planet, which is Mars. If you're just an ordinary man with nothing in your life, it's time to be smart. If you want to stay on Earth, you'll never know what's inside the universe. You should focus your perspective over the planet Earth. If one focuses only on what is in the world, one cannot see the beauty of life. You must discover the entire universe before you're gone.

※※※

In the recent update from
The Washington post

Dutch Non-profit Mars One has named 100 people who will stay in the running for a one-way trip to Mars; expected to leave Earth in 2024. Out of over 200,000 applicants, 24 will be trained for the mission. Another four will take the first trip; if all goes according to plan.

This round of eliminations was made after Norbert Kraft. The chief medical officer of Mars One interviewed 660 candidates who said they would leave everything behind to venture into Mars. Applications were available to anyone over 18 years of age. Because the organization believes that its greatest need is not to find the smartest or the most skilled people, but rather the people who are most devoted to the cause.

Don't focus on the place where you always failed.

When I was younger, I've been stranded everywhere; no one notices me either. I'm walking on the street for how many miles with my guitar. They look at me as a different person. They still think I'm crazy, since I only hold my guitar the whole time. They're laughing because I'm different. Somehow, I laugh because they are all the same. Sometimes I think that their mind is too critical. I notice how their brain works while playing with my strings; sitting in the gutter, while looking under the moon. They pointed at me, but they didn't clean their hands. I still think it's so difficult when you're alone and no one's helping you. You need someone to be with, but no one likes you as you're just an ordinary man. For some, you're just only a waste. I realized in those days, it's so awful when you're poor because nobody like you. Wherever I go, I am alone; my only friend is my guitar. Most people hate you when you're nothing. I realize that if you have something to give, everyone wants to make a friend of you. But if you have nothing, no one likes to be with your friend. I promise myself that if I get rich, I will never return to where I came from again. I focus only on those who give me value. The people that I meet right now are my very important people in my life. I don't want to see the people that I've met before who tell me negatively. Saying, "Be normal," or "You're weak." These words, "You can't do it," and "Give up." But being abnormal, sometimes, you will know the course of life.

If people are doubting how far you can go, go so far that you can't even hear them anymore.

Powerful Advice

Friends, if you want to live something new, go to another place where you find your happiness. Don't stick your old life. You need to explore. If you keep going back where you are, you will not find yourself. Find the real meaning of life; here you can enjoy. Do not focus on where you are struggling with. Leave the place where you can start over. If you always repeat on your routine, you go circling on your life until you die. The universe is vast, you should explore it. Try different things in your life, with nobody controlling you; anything that you can't possibly think you can't. It can happen if we can do something different. Happiness comes from exploring new things. You cannot explore a big thing in life if your perspective is only small. If you want to see yourself creating a big thing, don't focus on the small things.

Rich Mindset Activity Action Exercise

1. Write and send a short letter or e-mail to someone you know (not necessarily personally) who is very successful in any area. Tell them how much they own this success.

2. Identify a situation or a person who is down in life. Remove yourself on that situation. If it's family, choose to be less close to them.

3. Choose the planet that you want to live in the future. Google it, and do an update of Kepler's space telescope.

4. What makes you want to live on the planet Mars? Be specific.

5. Bend your arm straight in front of you and make a fist in your hand and say this:

I will become rich!

One more time.

I will become rich!

One more time.

I will become rich!

say it again and again.

How poor people struggle with their behaviours?

"Poverty is the parent of revolution and crime."
— Aristotle, Greek philosopher

Poor people have always something to say.

Two happy couples riding a donkey, but have two spectators.

- When two couples riding a donkey.

They say, "Two people on the donkey. Poor animal."

- When woman gets down to the donkey.

They say, "How cruel he is by letting his wife walk."

- When the man goes down to the donkey and places his wife on board.

They say, "How stupid he is by letting his wife take a ride alone."

- When two couples' dismount.

They say, "Fools! Don't even know how to utilize the donkey?"

Poor people always have something to say; just ignore them and enjoy the ride

"Whoever oppresses the poor, shows contempt for their Maker, but whoever is kind to the needy honors God."

— Proverbs 14:31, NIV

Why is it that the poor are believed to be poor because of their bad choices?

Inspiring Story

The Story of Cecilia Mo

Cecilia Mo believed she knew everything about poverty when she started teaching at Thomas Jefferson High School in southern Los Angeles. As a child, she remembered standing in line and having a free lunch ticket. As it turned out, Mo could always be shocked by poverty and violence; especially after a 13-year-old student called her in obvious panic. He had just seen his cousin get shot in his front yard.

For Mo, hard work and a good education took her to Harvard and Stanford. But when she saw how her LA students faced chaos and violence, she acknowledged how fortunate she was to have grown up with educated parents. Live in a safe, and financially stretched home.

Now, as an assistant professor of public policy and education at Vanderbilt University, Mo is studying how to get America's upper class to recognize the benefits they have. She is part of an academic group that is trying to understand how the rich and the poor justify inequality. What these academics are discovering is that the American dream is being used as a justification for a national nightmare.

The Fundamental Attribution Error

Hard work and good education were a safe bet for upward mobility in the United States—at least among some groups of people. Americans born in the 1940s were 90% more likely to achieve economic success than their parents. Not likely, those born in the 1980s had only a 50/50 chance of doing it.

As the dream has faded, however, its effects have not. Several elements of normal psychology, combine to keep much in the economic specter. It convinced that the rich and the poor deserve what they obtain with exceptions made, of course, primarily for themselves.

This error "lays the foundation for beliefs that would tend to justify systemic inequity ," says Arnold Ho, principal investigator for the psychology of an inequality lab at the University of Michigan.

Why poor people are stuck from the poverty?

From my perspective, the media is the main cause of an issue, why people are stuck in poverty. As a result of the music they listen to, the telenovela they watch every day, the news and other social media they watch every day. Most people's problem right now, they always believe in what they've seen and what they hear. They will not seek another source of truth; what they hear from artist is what they believe; the celebrity that they love; the host that they expect them to become rich; the newscaster that they thought about bad news every day.

They believe that this personality was always telling the truth. Thus, they did not realize that these famous celebrities they admire did not care for them. It's the other way around on television. But as a matter of fact, how do you think they care if they don't know you personally? They didn't know that they only control by these people. Their mind is stuck in poverty because on the basis that they have seen on TV; the rich are always bad and evil. They always realize that the poor are always oppressed by the rich. That's why they hate making money because they think being rich is evil and bad; according to what they've seen every day on TV. Now, for what they believed, they still accuse the rich. Reason why they are so poor. However, they're still sitting on the couch looking at Telenovela every day. The only thing they know is by hating the rich; thinking that the rich are only the problem. But in reality, their attitude is still the problem.

Cycle of Poverty

According to Wikipedia, in economics, a poverty trap or cycle of poverty is caused by self-building mechanisms that cause once it exists; it persist unless there is external intervention. It can last from one generation to the next, and when applied to developing countries, it is also known as a development trap.

Controversial educational psychologist Ruby K. Payne, author of A Framework for Understanding Poverty, distinguishes between situational poverty, which can generally be traced to a specific incident within the lifetimes of the person or family members in poverty. Generational poverty, which is a cycle that passes from generation to generation, and goes on to argue that generational poverty has its own distinct culture and belief patterns.

The Economics of Poverty.

With the new Global Goals agreed this autumn (UN 2015), the issue of poverty is at the top of global agenda. In a new book, The Economics of Poverty: History, Measurement and Policy, it reviews past and present debates on poverty in rich and poor countries.

The book strives to provide an accessible synthesis of economic thinking on key questions:

- ❖ How is poverty measured?
- ❖ How much poverty is there?
- ❖ Why does poverty exist?
- ❖ What can we do to reduce and eliminate that?

According to the Brooking's Report

The belief that lacks of income is the central issue of entrenched poverty. It also encourages continued emphasis on cash social assistance; a strategy that has not been successful. The average welfare check of about $400 per month (not including food stamps) can prevent destitution. However, it is not sufficient to eliminate a typical family of three from poverty. Even if it were to succeed, it may not improve the chances of survival for the children of those families; unless other changes occur. In her book: What Money Can't Buy, Susan Mayer argued that children in higher income families do better in school and experience fewer behavioral problems than those in lower-income families. This is not because their families have more income, but because they have better parents. In other words, adults who do better financially tend to have a variety of other characteristics that provide benefits to their children. The reason hasn't been widely recognized because most studies (Mayer's is the exception) have not been able to adjust for all of these parental differences. Some of them, such as encouraging children to do well in school, providing them with a structured routine, reinforcing good behavior, or just having good genes, are very hard to measure.

None of this means that providing more money for lower income families is necessarily a bad thing. But we should not claim that money alone will make a significant difference in the lives of these families beyond alleviating certain difficulties. The challenge is to find ways of providing generous support to the poor without disregarding the unpleasant facts about their behavior. Ideally, we need to nudge them toward a different set of behaviors by linking generous governmental assistance to staying in school, delaying childbearing, getting married, and working full-time.

Rich Mindset Activity Action Exercise

1. Find ways to minimize your entertainment consumption. It's better not to care about the celebrity's life. Instead, focus on yourself by building your wealth.

2. Stop following the celebrity that you admire. Focus only on following the people who can help you become rich. Remember, you don't get anything from the celebrity. Don't waste your time for them.

3. Bend your arm straight in front of you and make a fist in your hand and say this:

I will become rich!

One more time.

I will become rich!

One more time.

I will become rich!

say it again and again.

How poor people suffer from hunger?

Only the rich can help the poor.

"It is the desire of God that you should get rich.

He wants you to get rich because he can express himself better through you if you have plenty of things to use in giving him expression.

—Wallace D. Wattles

In life, some persons owe a lot in their life, but have little contribution to others. But some people may not have much in life, but contribute too much to others. Some individuals are too fond of money, but others are too hungry to feed themselves. There's nothing wrong with wanting a lot of money, because we need money to eat, to buy the things we need, and most importantly, to create wealth for your family. Although, we also believe this is why we made money to help others. Most people's problem they preferred not to help so that they do not lose money. Anyway, if you believe in the theory of helping and giving, your money will be multiplied by how much more you will earn. The capitalists can earn more money purchase by giving more value to others and to the church. The capitalist investor is the top of the world. In this world of high-speed technology, it is easier than ever to be capitalist in a world of overabundance. Remember, real

capitalists are generous, because they know when to give more in order to receive.

Did you know that?

Hundreds of millions of pesos of aid and rehabilitation funds did not reach the victims of Super Typhoon Yolanda in 2013. As government offices used it for operations or kept it in banks.

In its assessment report, the Audit Commission (COA) stated that the OCD had a total of 692,770,000 pesos—available for 2013. Whereas the NDRRMC, which is administered by the OCD, had received a total of 48. 82 million pesos in donations for the victims of the typhoon.

I remember that my friend, who was from Leyte during the typhoon, was among the victims of the tragedy. He told me that whenever he swims to survive, many dead bodies float before him. He'll be looking for someone to hang onto so he doesn't get swept away. Every time he will see the people breathing to survive under the water, he will force himself to take a very deep breath to push himself over the surface of the water so that he may survive (as his arms swung toward the floating house). When the rain has disappeared after one hour in the house, the strong wind is closest to its enemy. As he clung to the house it was slowly blown away by the wind. So, he was forced to jump underwater again, for he's not windblown away.

Once the typhoon is over his next enemy is starvation. He finds ways to eat food. He was gradually starving to death. No one helped them right away because no one respond immediately. They feel like zombies that they want to eat their flesh for survival, while his other comrade cry because their loved ones are dead. For several days, he was hungry before he was able to eat. He said that he will never forget that tragedy in his whole life; even when he is old. After that he realizes, it's so difficult if you're just

a poor person; you can't escape immediately if anything bad happens. But her other friend, with money, escaped just before the tragedy.

After this event, he went to Manila to find jobs. For he never wants it to happen again. He has learned that the government cannot be expected to act. He now works in a fast food restaurant and lives happily with his wife in Manila.

According to the Borgen Magazine

The biggest challenge to access food in the Philippines is the lack of income as a result of unemployment. This problem is particularly prevalent in the southern island region of Mindanao: where nine of the 16 poorest provinces are located.

In the Muslim Mindanao, which more recently serves as a battlefield between the ISIS-affiliated Maute group and the Philippine military soldier. About 50% of the population live below the national poverty line; earning only 60 cents a day. Those who reported food insecurity in this area reported a lack of income (37%), lack of regular employment (18%) and droughts and natural calamities (12%) are the primary reasons for hunger.

Malnutrition in the Philippines

Hunger is one of the extreme effects of poverty in the Philippines. With a small amount of money to buy food, Filipinos are forced to survive on very little food. Even when food supplies are stable, they are most accessible in other areas where people have enough income to purchase the food.

With such an unequal distribution of income, there is limited demand for food supplies in less developed areas; home of low-income residents. The quality of food is also decreasing. Rice was once the primary food source for Filipinos, but now it has largely been replaced with instant noodles, which is cheaper but less nutritious. As a result, malnutrition has become a lot more common.

"Americans are blessed with great plenty;

we are a generous people and we have a moral obligation to assist those who are suffering from poverty, disease, war and famine."

— Adam Schiff, U.S. representative

In the recent news of Yahoo News

The United States says that $6 billion of the world's billionaires could solve the present hunger crisis. Elon Musk says that he will sell the Tesla shares and donate the proceeds if the UN can prove it.

Musk was responding to comments by David Beasley, director of the UN's World Food Program, who told CNN's Connect the World last week that a $6 billion donation from billionaires like Musk and Bezos could help 42 million people who are "literally going to die if we don't reach them.

Hunger is not the problem.

You are the problem.

I remember when I was young, I got a friend who was very poor. His parents are in a low-income family. They invited me to eat with them once, they asked me so many questions, like: how big was your house? How much money do your parents earn? Are you studying in a private school? I have noticed that the topic of a poor people at the table is always whether other people's lives are good, and then blame their children for their misfortune. They never knew how to thank the grace of God. They envy others' lives because they have less in their lives. I am not blaming them because I understand that the provinces can only obtain a very low income. However, I notice here in Manila that the attitude of the poor and those in province are the same; although there are plenty of opportunities here. No matter where else you live, but if your mind is lazy, you're stuck with your attitude. That's why some people in the province went to Manila to have a better life. Some people want to communicate on a random basis in Manila to escape poverty. As well as Manny Pacquiao, he was born in Kibawe, Bukidnon and grew up in General Santos, Philippines.

At the age of 14, Pacquiao moved to Manila, where he lived in the streets. He worked as a construction worker and had to choose between enduring hunger or sending money to his mother. He began boxing and made the National Amateur Boxing Team of the Philippines where his room and board were paid by the government.

Hunger is not the barrier to make your lives better; the hindrance is your attitude to make you hungry. There are people who have less, but they find ways of improving their lives. If you always think that hunger is the only solution to your situation—to not find ways to escape from starvation. You always get hungry for the rest of your life. If you could spend the rest of your life worrying about your situation, that chapter will remain forever.

Don't be content with what you have right now because our lives have limitations. Thus, our dreams are limitless. You can do whatever you want to do in life; no one can stop you from fulfilling your dreams. The only problem that can stop you is yourself, because you cannot find a solution to your problem.

In the Report of Chicago Booth

U.S. lawmakers have expressed frustration when investments such as welfare programs do not lift people out of poverty. "I believe in helping those who cannot help themselves, but would if they could," said Senator Orrin Hatch (Republican of Utah) this past December, when explaining his views on government spending. "I have a rough time wanting to spend billions and billions and trillions of dollars to help people who won't help themselves, won't lift a finger, and expect the federal government to do everything."

Hatch's statement reflects a shared view that withdrawing government support would force many poor people to make their own improvements. Without welfare and government assistance, would able-bodied people find a job, get an education, stop buying lottery tickets, and focus on paying bills?

In a 2013 study published in Science, researchers from the University of Warwick, Harvard, Princeton, and the University of British Columbia find that for poor individuals, working through a difficult financial problem produces a cognitive strain. That's equivalent to a 13-point deficit in IQ or a full night's sleep lost. Similar cognitive deficits were observed in people who were under real-life financial stress. Theirs is one of multiple studies suggesting that poverty can harm cognition.

"You can't get rid of poverty by giving people money."

— P.J. O'Rourke, political satirist

Rich Mindset Activity Action Exercise

1. Pamper yourself. For at least once a month do something to nurture your spirit. Get a massage or manicure. Grab yourselves some lunch or dinner. Grab a milk tea or read books on Starbucks. You may need to connect with family or a friend. Give yourself a reward. Do things that will allow you to feel rich.

2. Make an envelope for tithing. Give at least 5% or 10% of your income to God.

3. Bend your arm straight in front of you and make a fist in your hand and say this:

I will become rich!

One more time.

I will become rich!

One more time.

I will become rich!

say it again and again.

Rich people have a good mentality. Poor people have a bad mentality

There are times when I feel that my neighbors have bad intentions. I notice that every midnight when I go out to get something to eat. People that hang around to stare at me

badly. It seems like they had something planned for me. I'm so scared because I'm the only one living in my apartment. I'm afraid to think that every time they might enter the house and stab me while I was asleep.

I have tried to convince them in a good way, but our thinking is different; we cannot reconcile. Some of them are members of the fraternities. Others are under the influence of something that might accommodate their minds. I always prayed to God that this person would never hurt me, because I don't have family here. Nobody will save me, whenever anything happens to me. I'm the only one who lives down here in Manila. I don't have any friends or relatives I can go near when I need help. Every day, I was scared to death. I always prayed to transfer into the subdivision area or into the condo with security outside the door. Every time I walk on the street during midnight, I thought that, "Please, Lord guide me no matter what happens. I have so many dreams. I don't want to die early. I've got mission to do. But if you want me to die for nothing, I will. It was painful, but I accept whether it's my destiny. Yet, please Lord, this is not my time."

I sense that these people hated me so much for the way I talk. I always talk to them about investing and how to make money as they approach me. They've always heard me talk about money, because I don't have anything to think about other than money. Whenever people ask me about things I do for a living. I say, "Nagpapayaman." (Making myself rich.) So maybe because of what I said, they're bragging about me. They feel like I'm so arrogant. Seeing as they think I feel rich. Perhaps there's nothing wrong with wanting a high, right? I think it's better to want something than not.

People will never understand me unless they join me into my world. The only person that can understand me is the rich people. I want to have something in life to be able to meet them in person, since that's my life. That is what God wants me to do: become rich and to meet those people who can understand me of what I am doing. Because these people that I meet every day, they will never understand what I've said. All they think about me is being weird, because I always care about money. They still think

I'm bad and greedy, as far as they're concerned, money is evil. Which is why they don't like me, because I'm an opportunist. I've always prayed to God every day that he will take me away from this people.

"Most people think that they want more money than they really do.

Still, they settle for a lot less than they could get."

-Earl Nightingale

According to Statistic Research Department

In 2018, approximately 23,600 incidents were reported for theft in the Philippines. Furthermore, crimes inflicting physical injury against other persons amounted to around 21,500.

Physical injury in the Philippines

Of all crimes against people in the Philippines, the infliction of physical injuries was the most serious; nearly 13,000 reported incidents in 2019. According to the Philippine National Police (PNP), physical injury is one of the top eight major crimes, including robbery and theft.

Teach your children by making money.

I remember my friend when I was a little kid, his job is to steal clothes around the house. I meet these children in the poverty area, because I've once slept in slums. Every day, this group of children plan to how to steal everything in someone's house. They will come into every house while the people sleep in the night. They will join forces by the group of gangs. Their job is to steal whatever they want to get in the house, and sell it to the market. Those children are lack of advice from their parents; just as my parents did. All they know is that robbery is normal and is part of their lives. Every day, when they go home, they bring clothes that they sell at a lower price. When they sold all the clothes, all the money they got is just spend it on buying a 'rugby'.

Unfortunately, these children know nothing but to destroy their lives. They thought the world didn't care about them. How can the world have forsaken these young people on the streets? It was like they were condemned by their soul. All they know is to take drugs at the young age. They have nobody to teach them education because their parents are uneducated. I hope the youth of today will hear from the government about their situation.

Kids are the only hope for our country so we can change our lives for the better. We have to guide them in the proper education, and teach them the value of money. When they were young, they had to know the importance of money. For if they had a proper education, they persevered for their lives. Before, I didn't care about money, since money wasn't the most important thing in my life. All I know about money is that I use it to play online games at an internet cafe, but I didn't know the value of it. I didn't know that money is the key to get out in poverty. If I only knew about money when I was a child, I could do a lot of good things. Yet the school never teaches us about money. Even if street kids have a lot of money, if they don't learn their value, they will spend it on drugs. Even if you make a lot of money, but if you do not know what you should buy, you will end up becoming an evil.

Sometimes money makes us bad if we don't have a proper education. If we teach our kids how to make financial literacy when they are young, they will become wiser when they grow up. If our children know at least little about money, they will no longer steal. If they can make a profit for themselves by selling something, they will no longer be on the street. They will see them on the market selling goods or anything. If their parents teach them how to set up their own businesses in the future, they will begin to learn how making money when they are young.

Kids are stealing, because they think they're having fun by getting money. However, they do not know how to make their own profit because, at an early age, they already know that money can buy everything. They find ways of getting money by stealing for something. If they have a proper education, they will pursue the value of their lives.

As a result, they have no clue about the value of their money. That's why they're still stealing, because all they know is that it's the only way they can get money.

Inspiring story

A Story about Ishaan Thakur and her sister, Aanya.

Fourteen-year-old Ishaan Thakur and her sister, 9-year-old Aanya, spent their summer building a profitable cryptocurrency mining company. Each month, the siblings make over $30,000 mining three digital coins. Bitcoin: the largest cryptocurrency by market value. [The second-largest is raven coin] Likewise, an altcoin amid the top 100.

"Crypto mining is just like mining for gold or diamonds," Ishaan says. "Instead of using shovels, you mine with computers. Instead of finding a piece of gold or a diamond in the mine, you find a cryptocurrency."

His parents were supportive. "We could have spent the entire summer playing video games, but instead we used our spare time to learn about technology," Ishaan added.

"On their first day, I made $3."

"We liked it so much that we started to add more processors [or chips], and made $1,000 in our first month of May," Ishaan says.

"In total, they expect to earn around $36,000 in September based on the equipment currently on order," Raj respond.

Kids are the only way to achieve a brighter future.

Does today's youth still hold the future of the country?

The answer probably lies in the system. If the increasing number of solvent and rugby sniffing youngsters roaming the streets in Quezon City and nearby areas is made the sole basis.

According to a Manila Bulletin

Quezon City resident Cesar Santos reported being a victim of rugby and solvent-sniffing beggars during heavy rains one night. As they detached the rear-view mirrors from his vehicle when he stopped for a red-light signal along Araneta Avenue.

In an interview on Kamias Road, one of the children who identified as 'Nini' admitted to sniffing solvent to relieve her hunger. whereas its companion known only as 'Totoy' says that the chemical gives it a different feeling of satisfaction.

Education System in the Philippines
On the Study of Future Learning

Most of the problems in the Philippines' education system from a lack of funding: low teacher salaries, a shortage of classrooms and lack of facilities such as laboratories. Additionally, there is a lack of educational equality between regions. Government policy tends to favor schools near Manila, with regions farthest from the capital (such as Mindanao) showing lower levels of student performance.

As with many other developing countries, one of

the main problems of the Filipino education system is the 'brain drain'; the departure of talented students, graduates and faculty overseas. Until home opportunities match the number of qualified graduates leaving the educational system; this seems to be an ongoing problem.

"Whatsoever things ye ask for when ye pray, believe that ye receive them, and ye shall have them," said Jesus

Rich Mindset Activity Action Exercise

1. Tell your kids one story at night before bed. Reading stories can help you maintain relations with your children. Stories encourage children to use their imagination and picture of the scenes in their head.

2. Educate your children about the importance of money, at a younger age. It's important to the kids on how to earn their own money. Encourage the kids to make money online.

3. By saving at a young age, kids can set aside funds that could help them in the future. Educate your children on saving and budgeting.

4. Bend your arm straight in front of you and make a fist in your hand and say this:

I will become rich!

One more time.

I will become rich!

One more time.

I will become rich!

say it again and again.

Poor people are vicious. Rich people have vision

Save the user. Jail the pusher.

According to The World's report dated July 2017.

The Bicutan Rehabilitation Center in Manila counts nearly 1,100 patients; twice its maximum capacity. At least 7,000 suspected drug users and pushers have been killed by police or unidentified vigilantes since July. Some of the victims include those who have voluntarily surrendered to the authorities. Many fear that implicating yourself might actually put you more at risk.

This premonition has reverberated throughout the country's rehab centers. It was here that drug addicts sought refuge from a seemingly inevitable death on the streets. Dealing with addiction is no longer the primary reason for dependent drug addicts to undertake rehabilitation.

My Story about Drugs

When I was 25, I was addicted to 'shabu', (methamphetamines) and marijuana. I began sniffing shabu and marijuana when I was 20. At first, it was natural for me, I was so excited every time I took drugs. Hanging out with my poor friends everyday feels like I'm not alone. Due to my loneliness and despair, I would prefer to be with them even though they are in trouble. I feel like I'm the only one, and nobody loves me. So, I went into a trance. When that happens, I want to have a wife. I want to have someone in my life, but I feel that no one likes me. Because of the grief of having someone to live, I chose a vicious person. I've done nothing, but become addicted every day. Used to spend all my money on drugs. I have no one to come near, but only those with vices. I used to like a woman in college, but I sense that she was afraid of me. I just suppressed my feelings for the better, even if I feel like she only disgusting to me. At that point, I want to settle down with someone, yet I have the impression that they hated me so much.

All I want then is to have a good friend who can speak out of my way. Despite everything, no one likes me to be a friend. They think I'm a bad person. They believe that I was a bad influence on their lives. Which is why they fear me and don't want me to be their friends. In this case, I wanted to focus on my study, still I can't. Each time my classmates saw me, I felt as if they hated me; although I do nothing to them. Even my teachers, they make me feel so disgusting. They look at me differently. Therefore, I realize that perhaps I wasn't born in school, because everyone in school

hates me so much. As a result, I am unable to focus

on my studies. There's a lot of people who make barriers to fulfilling my dreams. The problem with people is that they only alter your life. Still, no one is going to help in goodness. They're just there to judge you, even though you're just totally quiet and doing nothing.

Every time I go to school, I keep silent and do nothing. And yet, the people inside my head do something. I do not know if it was the effect of the drug. You thought that someone whispered to you, but the truth is, no one. It is only your imagination. This is why I can't concentrate on my study; I've been distracted by the noise in my head. That's the moment I realize that I'll never go back to school again, since I don't fit in there. I can't find what I'm looking for here. It cost me a lot of money, but I never got the degrees. School hates me a lot, but other things that matter in life are not. So, I focus my attention on what's important. I just thought that I can only recover from my expenses in school if I work hard now.

Powerful Advice

Friends, stop taking drugs for it will destroy your mind. Your mind was distracted and you felt like people would judge you; that's the effects of drugs. You thought someone was whispering to you, yet that was your imagination. It keeps you out of people; it is the side effect of drugs. Don't waste your life, as your mind has made fun of you. You can't concentrate in your life, because you thought everybody around you was whispering. But it was only your mind; the only enemy you can't get out of here before you quit drugs. Promise, I've done that thing. You know that the hardest enemy of us is ourselves, for it was difficult to break these bad habits. You against yourself, and it was the hardest opponents of all. Don't listen on your mind that thought you as an evil. It's a way of getting addicted, you open your mind to other dimensions.

On the Study of Cypress Lake Lodge

A gateway drug is a substance that leads to the use of a more potent one. Marijuana has been labelled as a gateway drug because people who use it often turn to harder drugs with more intense euphoria. Alcohol and nicotine are also gateway drugs. Many adolescents start with alcohol and nicotine and eventually progress to more harmful drugs.

In an article from Joann Loviglio (2018), ABCNews states, "The higher the users experience depends on what they're really getting. Many users who want embalming fluid often get it with phencyclidine (PCP) mixed in."

A 1998 study by the Texas Drug Abuse Control Committee said, "Effects of embalming fluid include visual and auditory hallucinations, euphoria, a feeling of invincibility, increased pain tolerance, anger, forgetfulness and paranoia."

Gateway drugs are usually the starting point to harder drugs. People who use marijuana are at high risk of using cocaine, heroin, or painkillers. Young teens often try marijuana and drink, resulting in an addiction to drugs and alcohol.

Rich Mindset Activity Action Exercise

1. If you or your loved ones are suffering from addiction. Consult a rehabilitation center near from you, or contact and search online help treatment for drug addiction.

2. If you want to re-build and get out of drugs, try to live in other cities, so you far away from your bad influence friends. And control yourself not to use again. Find jobs, meet other good people that can remove you from doing drugs. Remember, you cannot quit your bad habits unless you don't remove yourself from the people that you use to be with doing that.

3. Bend your arm straight in front of you and make a fist in your hand and say this:

I will become rich!

One more time.

I will become rich!

One more time.

I will become rich!

say it again and again.

Poor people are immature. Rich people are matured

Poor people are very annoying.

I have noticed that the poor always find ways of bothering you; even if you treat them well. They come up with ways just to insult you. They do anything to make you angry. If you treat them the right way, it will make their insult even worse. Instead of making peace and being friends with you because you show humility, they will often insult you hard, and show off arrogant.

The problem of a poor people is that if you treat them well, they will treat you poorly. If you treat them bad, they will treat you good. The problem of today's society is that, if someone is trying to be humble, they are the only ones to be ashamed. If he is always an arrogant, he is the one who will be respected. It was like the mind of people right now are strange. Whatever you throw at a person, the contrary will happen. The most caused of a crime is incomprehension. This is the main factor that can caused problem to a society. If we can be generous, we can solve our problems easily. Though, we are not united. We only want to be in trouble.

Pride is everything we know to avoid losing; it is higher than our dignity. Poor people are always in search of a problem about you, and sometimes they will be insulted by others. It doesn't matter what they say just so you feel bad for others. Sometimes you will be shocked that other people look at you differently. You have no idea they'll tell them everything about your bad attitude; even if that's not true.

This is why poor people do not grow up, for they always focus on the way to collect your bad attitude. That's seems collecting and throwing to a person that is closed to you. They will not save their stones by building their own empire. Otherwise, it is the rich people who gather the stones they throw to build an empire.

On the Study of WebMD

Immature people lack some emotional and social skills; have a hard time connecting with other adults. Certain behaviors can indicate that this is an emotionally immature person.

Demanding Attention

Young children get bored when people don't pay attention to them. They'll do things to draw the focus back to themselves, even if that means acting out in negative ways. Emotionally immature adults often do the same. They might not act out in negative ways, but they may inject themselves into conversations or crack inappropriate jokes to get everyone's attention.

Avoidance Behavior

Immature people may not know the future or how to plan it. Refuses to accept significant responsibilities such as committed relationships, careers or investments. As well, home ownership is a sign of avoiding responsibility. People like that could let others care for them well beyond the point where they should be self-sufficient. It's sometimes called Peter Pan syndrome: based on the fictional character who never wanted to grow up.

Rich people play the game to win.

Poor people play not to lose.

Poor people are not growing, because they're focusing on how they will not lose. They're not concentrating on the way they can win. If they can win this competition, they are proud and show that their opponents are shameful. However, if the rich win, the poor will lose their temper. They're showing jealousy—finding ways to make you feel like a loser. But for rich people, if someone wins, they just support their opponents. As they believe that they lose because his ability is not enough to win the competition. Accepts their mistakes as they need more improvement and practice to win. They're showing empathy, optimistic and generosity even if they lose. They're acceptable, and learn from mistakes. But the poor don't agree to lose, because they always want to win. If someone falls down, they will say, "YES!" Thus, if they are the ones who fall, they will say, "NO." They are happy if someone does not succeed, because they want to win all the time. So, for the rich, if somebody falls, they're going to grab their hand because they want everybody to win. In any event, if they are the ones who will lose, they stand up and fight; learn from their mistakes. Reason why they become successful.

Rich people understand why poor people are so arrogant. They understand that the only ability of a poor people is to draw attention to others. Unlikely, rich people don't need any attention from others. Their only care is how to make other people's win. The rich know that if anybody else wins, they win as well. That's how a leader act. They ensure that others support one another. That is why they are always happy even if they lose or not. For they know that life don't always make you win. They will make you lose, before you win.

Why you need to remove yourself from unsuccessful people?

If you meet people who are not succeeding right now, remove yourself from these people as soon as possible. He doesn't have anything to do with you other than laugh. Sometimes, it makes you feel crazy and bad. I have had many experiences with these people, they will only make you feel like you are idiots. I went through this when I was singing at the local bar. The owner of the bar where I used to sing, he helped me nothing but to oppress me. Such people will not be respected in society, because they have done nothing but worsen your problem.

That's why they always fall, because they don't get any help. People still expect so much of themselves, but the only capacity they have is to fail others. That's how the karma sets in. What you throw to people will be returned to you. Hence, they will never succeed, because all they want is not to lose; while others who fail. They are chaotic. They hate people. They don't enjoy being with good people. All they want themselves to surround with a bad person; they have enjoyed being evil. This is why God does not want me to succeed in music, because He protects me from bad and evil. These people are not growing. They have everything in life, but lack of generosity. Only anger prevailed; only hate is known. Unsuccessful people never win in life; they are just destroying it. They are harming society; only exist for themselves. They're selfish and insecure. All they know is to be at the top. There is no change in them, unless they open their hearts to others.

Be careful who to share your plan.

Not everyone can be trusted. Sometimes the people closest to you are the ones who stab you back. Be careful who to share your income, relationship and plan. At times people act like they're helping you, but deep down, they're planning something bad for you. You may not see the truth in the face of a man. There are times when the people you believe whose best is the one whose heart is full of evil. The humanity of a person you can't see out of a human form; it was seen inside of a human's heart. Not everyone likes your idea, the others are pretending to have your plan. The only person who you can trust is 'you'.

At times, it is better not to talk to everyone, as your opinion is better than others. There are those who have too many opinions, but all of them are nothing. Don't listen to others opinion; people are always telling you lies. Instead, hear your own opinion. Since, the only knowledge of the people is that how they can defeat you. All the poor people know is how they can murder you; be careful with your bright intelligence. Sometimes it can put you in danger. There are people who have so much wealth that they use it to destroy people. They don't want other people to get an advantage, which is why they're finding ways to make you die.

Don't be blind to someone's kindness. Perhaps you won't know too much about your faith. Don't hope for what you give; not everyone has a heart like you. Sometimes the only people that love you the best are the ones that destroy you the most. Remember that addiction to person is more like addiction to a drug. Some of the nicest people are the ones who hurt the most.

People say they're happy with you, but they're only happy with what you have. You don't need to live everybody in the world. Sometimes our life can be a lot happier when we're alone. It's better to be alone than to surround yourself with the people you don't understand.

"Sometimes the journey has to be travelled alone in order to appreciate the strength that lie deep inside of you."

-Steven Aitchison

196

Rich Mindset Activity Action Exercise

1. Bend your arm straight in front of you and make a fist in your hand and say this:

I will become rich!

One more time.

I will become rich!

One more time.

I will become rich!

say it again and again.

Poor people focus on reading social media posts.
Rich people focus on reading books.

Poor people have a lot of drama.

Rich people have a lot of dollars.

One study shows that, since this is a relatively new technology, there is little research to establish the long-term consequences; both good and bad of using social media. However, many studies have found a strong connection between heavy social media and a heightened risk of depression, anxiety, loneliness, self-harm and even suicidal thoughts.

Inadequacy about your life or appearance.

Even if you know that the pictures you see on social networks are manipulated, they can still make you feel insecure about how you look or what's going on in your own life. Similarly, we all know that others tend to share just the highlights of their lives; rarely the low points that everyone experiences. But this does not lessen these feelings of envy and dissatisfaction. When you scroll through photos of a friend from their tropical beach vacation or read about their exciting new promotion in the workplace.

Isolation

A study at the University of Pennsylvania found that high usage of Facebook, Snapchat, and Instagram increases and decreases feelings of loneliness. Conversely, the study found that reducing social media usage can actually make you feel less lonely and isolated and improve your overall wellbeing.

Depression and Anxiety

Human beings need face-to-face contact to be mentally healthy. Nothing reduces stress and boosts your mood faster or more effectively than eye-to-eye contact with someone who cares about you. The more you prioritize social media interaction over in-person relationships, the more you're at risk for developing or exacerbating mood disorders such as anxiety and depression.

Why human interaction is gone?

When I was younger, my friends and I used to hang out. We can't talk right, because all we do is look at our phones. We do not focus on ourselves and communication has been lost. Instead, we are ignoring each other and focusing on our phones. We both sit at the same table, but we don't talk anymore. We prioritize the social media. It was like people aren't satisfied with their relationships in real life.

Social media is the number one cause for which the connection between them has gone. Humans no longer interact, which is why people are apart from each other. Because the connection of us was gone, we're not focusing anymore on each other. That's why most of our relationships no longer exist, because our current focus is on social media. What else did you learn on social media? What have you learned about the lives of other people? Are you getting rich if you follow them? What are the benefits of people you did not know on social media that your friends and relatives around you?

I've also used social media before. But now I'm focusing more on Google; seeking an important lesson in life. If I use social media, I use it to look at the motivational vlog, looking at cryptocurrency, the stock market and other investment shows. Some people who use social media are more focused on the lives of others. What have you got on the lives of others? Are they advising you on how to expand your assets? Are they teaching you how to increase your passive income, or they just show you how good life they have? Does your life turn beautiful when you watch them, or you just become insecure on their lives? because your current life is the same as your previous life and it does not change. Why not focus on how your life can be better, rather than focusing on the lives of others. What do you get by being heartfelt on other people's life? Have you ever earned money from it? Why don't you focus on reading books, instead of watching other people's lives? You're wasting your time for them. They will not help you to get rich.

Some kids nowadays are posting their parents together. However, in reality he didn't helped his mother on their housework. His face is still on his phone, but he never assisted his mother even on cleaning their plate. We always put a good life on the internet, but in reality, their life is a struggle; their life is lonely. He's proud of his social media profile, but actually, he's not proud of himself. He hates himself. Everyone is struggling, but they are showing the opposite of their lives on social media.

How Social Media is Reshaping Today's Education System?

"The best teachers I've ever had have used technology to enhance the learning process, including Facebook pages and events for upcoming projects"

—Katie Benmar

"We live in a digital ecosystem, and it is vital that

educational institutions adapt."

Empowering Effects

Starting from elementary school up until university graduation, social media has the role to empower parents, students and teachers to use new ways of sharing information and build a community. Statistics show that 96% of the students that have internet access are using at least one social network. What's even more extraordinary is that, even though some of the students use the social networks for entertaining and other purposes, there are a lot of them that actually use it to promote a lot of positive and useful activities. From finding a summer internship, promoting a success story about how to win the student-loan battle or collaborate on international projects, everything is made possible.

Implementation in Schools?

From a social media perspective, schools tend to take different positions. There is widespread agreement that they are useful when it comes to sharing information or organizing school tasks. At the same time, social networking is blamed for the lack of attention among students during courses.

Carla Dawson – Digital Marketing Professor at the Catholic University of Cordoba. Professor Dawson really has a valid point there as history has shown us that no matter how strong the resistance, technological progress and new trends will eventually become a standard. Of course, this applies to developed countries that already have a well-structured traditional educational system. It's a totally different situation when it comes to developing countries that are still struggling to find their way.

WAYS TO AVOID SOCIAL MEDIA DISTRACTION

SCREEN TIME – RESTRAIN YOURSELF & PARENTAL CONTROL

Available in the Play Store for Android.

Features:

1. App Daily Usage

➢ Shows a detailed view of your daily mobile phone usage.

2. App Weekly Usage

➢ Checks the statistics of your mobile phone usage in the last week and shows your daily usage trends.

3. App & Category Limit

➢ You can set a daily duration limit for each app or type of app and even a different duration for each day.

4. App Always Allowed List

➢ Pick which apps are important for usage and

whitelist them so the use of these apps will no longer be restricted.

SCREEN TIME

Features:

1. App Limits

➤ You can set daily limits for app categories with App Limits.

2. View your Report and Set Limits

➤ Screen Time gives you a detailed report about how your device is used, apps you've opened, and websites you've visited.

3. Downtime

➤ When you schedule downtime in Settings, only phone calls and apps that you choose to allow are available.

4. Always Allowed

➤ You might want to access certain apps. Even if it's downtime or if you set the All Apps & Categories app limit.

Rich Mindset Activity Action Exercise

1. Look at your child's eyes to see whether he is following the screen. Check if they're taking notes or zoning out. Ask questions at the end of a lesson.

2. Consider limiting your children's mobile phones and tablets until their school work is completed to their full attention.

3. Make sure your kids take plenty of breaks to get physical activity and time off the screens. Set up alarms similar to the ones they would meet at school and encourage them to stand up; get some fresh air, go for a walk or bike ride, or have a snack so that they are not sedentary for the entire day.

4. Face-to-face interaction is great for children, but as long as they don't return to school safely, encourage your children to video chat or text message rather than simply scrolling through social media.

5. Bend your arm straight in front of you and make a fist in your hand and say this:

I will become rich!

One more time.

I will become rich!

One more time.

I will become rich!

say it again and again.

Hopefully, this whole lesson of this book will help you change the way you think and you can apply it to your everyday life. Read it constantly until it gets into your subconscious mind. Follow all the activities I propose with this book to change your lifestyle. This will help you on your journey to financial freedom.

Sincerely yours,

Jo Batiquin

About the Author

Jo Batiquin

Jo Batiquin is a thirty year old entrepreneur and musician from Cebu city but lives in the Manila now. He enjoys spending time writing books and singing songs.

Follow me on:

https://www.facebook.com/groups/189198873167671

https://www.instagram.com/thebestjome/

https://www.youtube.com/channel/UCY09fPv7daF2stABifS3 6pQ

https://www.pinterest.ph/jbatiquin12345/_saved/

https://www.linkedin.com/in/jo-batiquin-780b68229/

Email me at: jbatiquin12345@gmail.com

www.ingramcontent.com/pod-product-compliance
Lightning Source LLC
LaVergne TN
LVHW041703070526
838199LV00045B/1173